SHAKER

SHAKER

DAVID S. MORGAN

HORIZON ECHO PUBLISHING

Copyright © 2026 by David S. Morgan All rights reserved.

This is a work of fiction. While inspired by Shaker communities in America, it is not based on any specific community, and all characters and events are imagined.

Horizon Echo Publishing.

Honoring Faith.

"Hands to work, hearts to God."
— **Shaker proverb**"

Table of Contents

Chapter One: The Road 1

Chapter Two: The Arrangement 15

Chapter Three: Roles 34

Chapter Four: Confession 55

Chapter Five: The Assessment 75

Chapter Six: The Long View 86

Chapter Seven: Adjustment 101

Chapter eight: Care 122

Chapter Nine: Doctrine 141

Chapter Ten: Labor 157

Chapter Eleven: Silence 176

Chapter Twelve: Absence 196

Chapter Thirteen: The Task 212

Chapter Fourteen: The Record 220

Chapter Fifteen: Joy 239

Chapter Sixteen: Fidelity 258

Chapter Seventeen: The Sealing 278

Chapter Eighteen: What Remains 287

Chapter Nineteen: Return 297

A Note on the Shakers: 305
Further Reading..306
Author's Note..307

CHAPTER ONE

The Road

They came into the valley from the east, where the road rose before dropping again into farmland. The late afternoon sun was behind them now, their shadows stretching long and thin on the asphalt ahead. Two riders. The man in front, the woman a bike-length behind. They had been riding for three hours, and the rhythm had settled into something automatic, the legs turning, the breath finding its own pattern.

The road here was narrower than the state highway they had left that morning. No shoulder. Stone walls ran along both sides; the stones stacked without mortar in the old way, gray and lichen-spotted, broken in places where trees had pushed through, or frost had done its slow work over decades. Beyond the walls, fields. Some still cut for hay, the stubble pale and uniform. Others gone to goldenrod and timothy, the tall grasses bending in the same direction under a wind they could not feel on the road. The air smelled of late summer going over into fall. Warm earth, dried grass, something faintly sweet that might have been apples from an orchard they had passed a mile back.

The man shifted to a lower gear. The grade had seemed flat, but his legs said otherwise. That slight resistance that accumulated over miles, the constant argument between body and terrain. His breathing was louder than he wanted it to be. He could hear her breathing too, steady, closer to the rhythm she had held since the second hour. Her cadence was more efficient than his. It had always been.

Neither of them spoke. They had talked earlier, in the first miles, the nervous energy of starting, the small observations about weather and road conditions that filled the space before effort made talking expensive. Then less. Then not at all. The silence was not uncomfortable. It was the silence of effort shared, of attention directed outward and inward simultaneously.

A crow lifted from a fencepost as they passed. Its wings made a sound like heavy fabric shaking. It crossed the road ahead of them and disappeared into the trees on the left. The trees were mostly maple and ash, some beech with their smooth gray bark, and beyond them the land rose toward hills that were beginning to catch the lower angle of the sun.

The road curved left around a stand of maples. The leaves were just beginning to turn, the edges going red while the centers held green, the color change starting at the margins, the way it always did. Another week, two at most, and the color would be full. They had timed it for this. The inn where they would stay that night advertised itself for leaf season.

Three more miles, according to the map they had studied at breakfast.

He saw the buildings first.

On the right, set back from the road perhaps two hundred yards. A cluster of them, large, white or pale yellow, arranged with a regularity that caught the eye. Not a farm. The structures were too big, too numerous, too deliberately placed. They stood on a slight rise, the land sloping gently up from the road, and in the late light they seemed to glow against the darker hills behind them. The glow was not supernatural. Just the particular quality of white paint in angled sunlight. But it drew the attention in a way that felt deliberate.

He did not stop. But he slowed. His cadence dropped, and he heard her adjust behind him, the click of her derailleur as she downshifted, the subtle change in the sound of her tires on the road.

The buildings were old. He could see that from the road, from the proportions and the way they sat on the land. Two, three stories. Wooden, with many windows, the windows tall and narrow with small panes. The windows caught the sun and gave nothing back, neither reflection nor glimpse of interior. Between the buildings, open spaces. Grass, very green, very even, the kind of green that came from consistent care. No vehicles that he could see. No signs of equipment or storage or any of the ordinary clutter of occupied places. Just the buildings and the grass and the careful emptiness between.

A white fence ran along the road. Not a working fence. Too low, too decorative, the posts too close together, and the rails too thin to restrain anything. It marked a boundary without enforcing one. Beyond it, a gravel drive curved up the rise toward the nearest building. The gravel was pale, recently maintained, raked smooth. No tire tracks that he could see from this distance.

He slowed further. He was not sure why. Something in the arrangement. The angles were too clean. The spacing too considered. It looked like a place that had been designed to be seen from this exact distance, from this exact angle, and from no closer.

The woman pulled up beside him. He heard her breathing change as she stopped pedaling. They coasted, losing speed gradually, the bikes making that soft ticking sound of freewheeling that always seemed louder in quiet places.

"What is it?" she said.

He did not answer immediately. He was looking at the nearest building. Three stories, a pitched roof, a small cupola at the peak with a weathervane that was not moving. The windows were arranged in rows, identical, each one the same size and the same distance from the next. There were many of them. Too many, it seemed, for the building to contain reasonably. As if the structure had been designed primarily to hold light, to collect it through all those small panes and do something with it that he could not imagine.

Through one of the lower windows, where the angle of the sun allowed it, he caught a glimpse of the interior. Just a flash. A floor, pale wood, worn smooth in a pattern he could not read from this distance. The wear was visible even from here. Not the random wear of foot traffic. Something more deliberate. Arcs, perhaps. Curves where straight lines should have been. Then the light shifted, and the window went dark again.

"I don't know," he said.

They had stopped now. Feet down, straddling the bikes, the frames still warm from the miles. His pulse was settling. The effort fog was clearing from his head. The wind touched the back of his neck where the sweat was cooling, and he felt the slight chill that came after sustained exertion when the body began to realize it had been working harder than the mind had registered.

The buildings did not move. Of course, they did not move. But there was something in their stillness that felt active. A quality of waiting. He had the sense, and it was only a sense, nothing he could have put into words or defended if pressed, that the structures were aware of him. That they had been aware of him before he saw them. That his attention, when it landed on them, had met something already attending.

He looked at the woman. She was looking at the buildings too. Her face was difficult to read in the shadow of her helmet. She had pushed her sunglasses up into her hair and was squinting slightly, the way she did when she was trying to see something that would not quite come into focus, some detail that kept sliding away from direct perception.

"It looks like a school," she said. "Or it used to be."

"Maybe."

But the buildings did not look like a school to him. They looked like something that had been completed. Not abandoned. Abandoned places had a different quality, a loosening, a surrender to entropy. These buildings looked maintained, cared for, their paint fresh and their windows intact. But completed in some other sense. As if the people who had built them had finished what they came to do and simply stopped. Left the structures standing because there was no reason to take them down and no reason to continue using them.

The wind moved through the grass on the rise. The grass bent and released, bent and released. The movement was regular, hypnotic. He watched it without blinking. The grass moved, but the buildings were still. The contrast made the stillness more pronounced, more deliberate.

"We should go," she said.

He heard her but did not respond. He was trying to identify what he was feeling. It was not fear, exactly. Not curiosity either, not in the usual sense. It was something physical, a tightness in his chest that had nothing to do with the miles they had ridden. An alertness. The way the body responds to a sound it cannot quite hear, to a presence it cannot quite locate.

The windows watched. He knew that was absurd. Windows did not watch. They were glass and wood and paint and nothing more. But the word came to him anyway, and once it came, he could not dismiss it. The windows watched, and he felt himself being seen, felt his presence on the road being registered by something he could not name.

The nearest building had a door, painted red. The red was faded now, weathered to a color closer to rust or dried blood. The door was closed. All the doors were closed, he realized, looking from building to building. Every door shut. Every window was dark despite the afternoon light. The buildings held their interiors hidden, offering nothing to the eye that was not surface.

"Peter," she said.

He turned. She had already started to roll her bike forward, one foot on the pedal, ready to push off. Her expression was patient, but there was something else in it too, something he recognized from other times when she had decided that a conversation or an observation had gone on long enough.

"We'll lose the light," she said.

It was true. The sun was lower than he had thought. The shadows of the buildings reached toward the road now, dark fingers spreading across the grass. In another hour, the valley would be in shade, and the temperature would drop quickly once the direct light was gone. They still had miles to cover.

He nodded. He clipped back into his pedal, felt the familiar resistance and release, the mechanical certainty of the connection. They started moving.

The road passed the cluster of buildings and curved gently to the right. He did not look back. He wanted to. Something in him insisted that he should, that failing to look back was somehow a concession he should not make. But he did not allow himself. The woman was behind him again, and he could hear her steady breathing and the soft sound of her tires on the asphalt, and that was enough. That was ordinary. That was what he needed.

The stone walls continued along both sides. The fields resumed. After a quarter mile, there was a farmhouse, white, with a red barn behind it, and he felt something loosen in his chest at the sight of it. A normal farmhouse. A normal barn. Trucks parked in the drive, their beds filled with firewood and fencing supplies. A dog asleep on the porch, lifting its head briefly as they passed, then settling again. The ordinary world, still present, still operating according to its ordinary rules.

They climbed a small rise. At the top, before the descent, he glanced over his shoulder. He could not stop himself. The buildings were still visible from here, smaller now, pale shapes against the darkening hills. From this distance they looked even more deliberate. A pattern placed in the landscape with intention. An answer to a question no one was asking anymore.

The woman pulled up beside him. She was looking too.

"Strange," she said.

The word did not seem adequate. He nodded anyway.

They began the descent. The road dropped faster than he expected, and he let the bike go, the wind in his face now, the speed building. The woman stayed with him. They leaned into a curve, and the landscape blurred at the edges, and for a moment, there was nothing but motion, the pure physical fact of bodies moving through space.

At the bottom of the hill, the road straightened and they eased back, letting their speed bleed off naturally. The effort of slowing, the tension in the brakes, the return of ordinary sensation. His legs remembered the miles. His shoulders ached where he had been gripping too tightly without noticing.

A sign appeared on the right: The inn. They turned onto a smaller road, gravel now, and the sound of their tires changed, became rougher, more present. The inn was a quarter mile down the road. A converted farmhouse, clapboard siding, a porch with rocking chairs. Normal. Welcoming. The windows were lit from within, and the light was warm and yellow and belonged to the ordinary world.

They dismounted and walked the bikes to the rack near the entrance. He stretched, feeling the pull in his lower back, the tightness in his calves. The woman was doing the same, rotating her neck, shaking out her hands where they had gone stiff from gripping the handlebars.

"That place back there," he said.

She looked at him.

"What about it?"

He did not know how to finish the sentence. He had started it without thinking, as if the words would come once he began. But they did not come. The sensation he had felt on the road was already fading, replaced by the ordinary concerns of arrival. The room. Dinner. A shower. The simple pleasures that followed a long ride.

"Nothing," he said. "Just strange."

She nodded. She did not press him. That was one of the things he appreciated about her. She understood that some things did not need to be explained. Some things simply were.

They went inside.

The innkeeper greeted them. Showed them to their room. The room was small and clean, with a view of the hills that were now dark shapes against a sky going purple at the edges. The woman showered first while he sat by the window and watched the light change. The last of the sun caught the highest peaks. A few early stars appeared.

He thought about the buildings. The arrangement. The stillness. The way the place had felt finished rather than abandoned. He thought about the windows and the faded red door and the grass bending in the wind. He thought about the word that had come to him unbidden: watching.

And the floor. That glimpse through the lower window. The wood worn smooth in curves that made no sense. He did not know why that detail stayed with him, but it did. Something about the pattern. Something about what could wear wood that way, over years, over decades. He could not picture it. He was not sure he wanted to.

The shower stopped. She came out, toweling her hair.

"Your turn," she said.

He stood. The window was dark now, reflecting his own face back at him. The hills were invisible.

In the shower, the hot water worked at his muscles. The steam filled his lungs. He stood under the spray for a long time, letting the miles wash away. When he closed his eyes, he saw the buildings again, but from a distance now, as if he were looking at a photograph of a place he had never been.

Later, at dinner, they talked about the route for tomorrow. The inn served good food, local, simple, and they ate more than they had expected. The wine was adequate. The other guests were pleasant. A retired couple from Connecticut. Two women who ran a pottery studio in Vermont.

No one mentioned the buildings on the road.

That night, in the dark, in the unfamiliar bed, he woke once. He did not know what had woken him. The room was quiet. The woman slept beside him, her breathing even.

He lay there listening.

After a while, he heard it. Or thought he heard it. A sound so faint it might have been inside his own head. A single note, sustained. Then another, slightly lower, as if in answer. Then silence. Then the first note again, fainter now, fading into something that was not quite sound but not quite silence either. Like a bell. Like two bells, calling and responding across a distance. Like the memory of bells that had stopped ringing long ago but had not yet finished being heard.

He listened until he was certain he had imagined it.

He was not certain.

He listened longer.

The sound did not return. Or if it returned, it had become so quiet that it was indistinguishable from the blood moving through his own ears, from the settling of the old inn, from the ordinary noises of night that the mind learns to ignore.

Then he slept.

In the morning, they rose early, ate breakfast, and paid their bill. The day was clear and colder than the day before. They dressed in layers. They checked their tires, filled their bottles, and clipped into their pedals.

The road out of the inn wound through woods for half a mile before joining the main route. At the junction, they stopped. Left would take them north, toward the coast, toward the rest of their planned route. Right would take them back the way they had come.

He looked right.

The road was empty. The morning light was flat and gray. The stone walls ran parallel, narrowing with distance. He could not see the buildings from here. The land curved, and they were hidden behind the bend.

"Ready?" she said.

He nodded.

They turned left.

The road climbed. The miles began to accumulate. By the time the sun was fully up, they were deep into the rhythm again, the steady effort, the steady breathing, the silence that was not uncomfortable.

He did not think about the buildings. He did not let himself. There was the road ahead, and the road was enough.

But somewhere in his body, in his chest, in his hands, in the place where physical memory lives below the level of language, he carried something he had not been carrying before. A weight that was not quite weight. A presence that was not quite presence.

The place remained.

Long after they passed out of the valley, long after the miles separated them from what they had seen, the place remained. Not as thought. Not as memory, exactly.

As fact.

A fact of the body. A fact that required no interpretation, no explanation, no understanding.

The buildings stood. The windows watched. The grass bent in the wind. The floors held their wear, their patient record of motion that had ceased but had not been erased.

And the road continued.

CHAPTER TWO

The Arrangement

The bell rang at half past four. In the women's dwelling, Ruth Harrow was already awake, had been awake for some time, lying in the dark and listening to the particular silence that preceded the day. The room held four beds. Two were occupied. The other two had been stripped to their ticking months ago, the linens folded and stored, the space left open because there was no reason to remove the frames themselves. The frames were well-made, oak, joined without nails in the manner that had been taught here for a hundred years. They would outlast their immediate usefulness.

The rooms were built for a number they no longer reached.

In the silence before the bell, she heard something. Or thought she heard it. A hum, low and constant, as if the building itself were holding a single sustained note. It was in the walls, perhaps. In the bones of the structure. She had noticed it before, on other mornings when she woke early enough to hear what the daylight hours obscured. She had never mentioned it to anyone. It was probably the blood moving through her own ears, the body's quiet machinery audible only when everything else fell still. She listened a moment longer, then let it go. The bell would ring soon. The day would begin.

She rose and dressed in the dark, her hands knowing the sequence without sight. Chemise, then the inner dress of plain cotton, then the outer dress of darker wool. Kerchief folded and pinned at the precise angle she had been taught when she first came here as a girl of nineteen. Cap fitted and tied, the strings crossing beneath her chin and secured at the back. She had performed this sequence thousands of times over forty-three years, and her fingers moved with the efficiency of long repetition. The sequence had been taught to her by Sister Patience, who had learned it from Sister Clarissa, who had learned it from one of the early ones. The early ones had dressed in the dark too, though for different reasons. They had needed the hours before dawn because the hours after meeting left them spent, emptied, their bodies recovering from what had moved through them. Ruth did not think of this as she dressed. She simply dressed. But the sequence carried what the sequence had always carried, passed from hand to hand across the generations, the muscle memory older than anyone now living.

Across the room, Sister Abigail stirred and began her own dressing. Neither spoke. Speech would come later, when there was reason for it.

The hallway was dim, lit only by the gray light beginning to show at the eastern windows. The windows were tall and narrow, set at regular intervals along the wall, each one the same size and the same distance from the next. Ruth walked the hall's length without hurry, her shoes making the soft sound they always made on the pine boards, boards worn smooth by decades of similar walking. The path of greatest wear was visible in the wood. A slightly lighter color where feet had traveled most often, a track that followed the center of the hallway and curved slightly toward the stairs. But the curve was not uniform. On the left side, the wear was deeper, as if generations of feet had once approached at angles the current residents no longer used. Ruth walked in the center, as she had been taught. She did not think about why the older wear pulled leftward. She simply walked where the walking was done now.

She passed four doors. Behind one, Sister Catherine was coughing. The cough she had carried since winter, neither better nor worse, simply present now, a condition to be accommodated rather than cured. Behind another, silence. The third and fourth rooms were empty now, had been empty since spring, but the doors remained closed as doors should be. Open doors suggested incompleteness, waiting. Closed doors suggested only that the rooms beyond them were not currently required.

The stairs descended in a single straight flight, eighteen steps, the railing smooth beneath her palm. Ruth took them as she always did, one hand on the rail, not from need but from habit, from the knowledge that rails existed for hands and hands should use them. There was a worn spot on the rail where thousands of hands had gripped it at the same point, turning the corner at the bottom. She gripped it there without thinking, her body remembering what her mind no longer needed to notice.

At the bottom, she turned left toward the kitchen. The hallway here was wider, built to accommodate the passage of pots and kettles and the occasional piece of furniture being moved for repair. The walls were whitewashed, as all the walls were, the whitewash renewed each spring in the same pattern it had always been renewed, room by room, the work distributed among those capable of doing it.

Sister Mercy was already in the kitchen. She had the fire built and the water heating, the oats measured into the great iron pot, the dried apples soaking in their crockery bowl. The fire was well-laid, the logs stacked to allow proper airflow, the kindling consumed, and the flames now settling into the steady burn that would last through the morning's cooking. Mercy was sixty-seven years old and had been doing this work for thirty-one years, and she did it well. When Ruth entered, Mercy looked up briefly, nodded once, and returned to her stirring.

"The preserves?" Ruth asked.

"Third shelf, left side. I moved them yesterday. The new jars are in back, the older ones in front, as you'd expect."

Ruth crossed to the pantry. The pantry was a narrow room lined with shelves, the shelves built into the walls at measured intervals, each shelf the same depth, each the same distance from the next. The organization was precise: dry goods on the upper shelves, preserves in the middle, root vegetables and heavier items below. The jars were orderly, each labeled in Sister Catherine's careful hand, the dates marked, the contents visible through the glass. Apple butter, dated September 1897. Pickled beans, August 1897. Tomatoes, September 1897. The colors were vivid behind the glass. Deep red, bright green, the amber brown of the apple butter. A record of the summer's work now stored against the winter's need.

She found what she needed, apple butter, enough for the morning, and brought it to the work table. The kitchen smelled of woodsmoke and warming oats and the particular clean smell of a space that was scrubbed daily and had been scrubbed daily for a hundred years. The scrubbing was not merely cleanliness; it was care, attention, the proper stewardship of tools and space.

The other women arrived in ones and twos over the next quarter hour. Sister Abigail came down and took her place at the bread station, her hands beginning the day's loaves without instruction. The bread dough had been set to rise the night before; now it needed shaping, dividing into the correct portions, each loaf the same size as every other loaf, because consistency was part of the craft. Sister Hannah entered quietly and began setting the tables in the dining room, her footsteps audible through the connecting door. Twelve steps to the sideboard, the soft clink of plates being lifted, twelve steps back to the table, the placement of each plate at its position. Sister Catherine appeared last, still coughing, and Ruth directed her to the lighter work of slicing bread, work that could be done sitting down.

"The butter is soft," Ruth said. "I set it out last night. It should spread without tearing the crust."

Catherine nodded and took her place on the stool that had been set beside the work table for exactly this purpose. Her hands were steady despite the cough. She had been here fifty-one years, longer than anyone except Ruth herself, and her competence had not diminished even as her lungs had. The knife moved through the bread in clean strokes, each slice the same thickness as the last.

By the time the second bell rang, five o'clock, the call to meeting, the kitchen work was organized and proceeding. The oats were thickening in the pot, the bread was sliced and arranged on platters, the apple butter had been transferred to the serving bowl, the water for tea was approaching its boil. Ruth wiped her hands on her apron and left the kitchen in Mercy's capable care, walking through the dining room where Hannah was finishing the last of the place settings.

Eight settings on the women's side of the room. The tables were long, built of maple, the surfaces polished smooth by years of use and cleaning. The plates were set at measured intervals, each one aligned with the edge of the table, each accompanied by its cup, its spoon, and its napkin folded in the way napkins had always been folded here. Twelve settings on the men's side, across the center aisle that divided the room, though Ruth knew that only nine would be filled this morning. Brother Daniel was in the infirmary. Brother Samuel and Brother Peter had both passed in the spring, within a month of each other. The extra settings remained because the number had always been twelve, and the tables had been built to hold twelve, and there was no purpose in removing what had been correctly made. The settings were not memorial; they were simply present, like the empty beds and the empty rooms.

The meeting room was on the first floor of the main dwelling, a large room with windows on two sides and benches arranged in rows facing the center. The benches were built into the walls in tiers, rising slightly toward the back, so that all could see and all could be seen. The floor in the center was open, polished wood, catching the early light that came through the eastern windows. The light moved across the floor as the sun rose, a slow tide that had been observed for a hundred years and would be observed for as long as the building stood.

The floor was worn here too, Ruth noticed. She noticed it every morning but did not think about it. The wear was different from the hallway's wear. Here, the wood was smooth in arcs and curves, worn not in paths but in patterns.

The patterns made no sense for a room where people sat on benches facing each other. They made no sense for walking, standing, or any ordinary use. Ruth had never asked about the patterns. She had been told, once, when she was young, but the explanation had been brief, and she had not thought to ask for more. The floor simply was what it was. It held its wear like a memory it did not need to explain.

The men entered through their door on the north wall, the women through theirs on the south. The two groups sat facing each other across the open space, the arrangement unchanged since the day the room was built. Ruth took her usual seat, third row, second from the aisle. The wood of the bench was smooth beneath her, shaped to accommodate sitting, worn by the same bodies returning to the same positions morning after morning.

The women filled in around her. Seven in all, including herself. Sister Mercy had remained in the kitchen to tend the meal, as she always did on mornings when she had the early duty. Across the space, the men took their places. Ruth counted without appearing to count: nine. Elder Thomas at the front, his white hair catching the light, his posture still straight despite his years. Brother William beside him, then Brother Joseph, then the others in their usual order, each man in the seat he had occupied for however many years he had been occupying it. Brother Daniel was not present. He had been unwell since Tuesday and was resting in the infirmary, which was proper. Rest was what the body required when the body was unwell, and the infirmary existed for exactly this purpose.

The meeting began with silence. This was how it always began. The silence was not empty but full, a shared attention that gathered the room into a single waiting. Ruth let her hands rest in her lap, and her eyes rest on the floor, and her mind rest in the quality of stillness that she had learned when she was nineteen years old and had practiced every morning since. The stillness was not absence; it was presence, a particular kind of presence that required nothing and offered nothing except the fact of itself.

In the silence, Ruth heard the hum again. Or thought she heard it. That low note, sustained, as if the building were breathing. As if the walls remembered holding something that vibrated at exactly this frequency. She let her attention settle on it, then released it. The silence continued. The hum, if it had been there, faded into the ordinary quiet of a room full of people not speaking.

Elder Thomas spoke first. His voice was clear despite his age. He was seventy-four now. His words were the words that opened every morning meeting, words that Ruth could have spoken herself if speaking had been her role. He spoke of the day's work, the tasks that needed attention, the orderly proceeding of labor that was both necessity and devotion. He spoke of Brother Daniel's condition, improving, the physician had confirmed, expected to return to light duties by week's end, and of the progress on the autumn preserving, which was now complete. Forty-seven jars of apple butter, thirty-two of tomatoes, twenty-eight of beans, and sixteen of corn relish. The numbers were part of the report, not because they needed to be celebrated but because they needed to be known. He spoke briefly and practically, without elaboration, because elaboration was unnecessary when the facts were sufficient.

When he finished, there was silence again. The silence was an invitation. Anyone could speak who felt moved to speak. This morning, no one did. The silence held for the span of several breaths, and then Elder Thomas nodded, and the meeting was complete.

The day's assignments had been posted the evening before, written in Ruth's hand on the slate board that hung in the hallway between the meeting room and the dining room. The board had hung there for forty years, its surface renewed each evening with the next day's arrangements, the chalk marks erased each night and rewritten each dusk. She had written them after supper, as she did each evening, consulting the ledger where all assignments were recorded and planning the next day's work according to need and capacity. This was her primary duty now: the keeping of the schedule, the arrangement of labor, the quiet accounting that ensured everything was done and everyone was placed where they could be most useful.

After breakfast, oats and bread and apple butter, eaten in the customary silence, the only sounds the small sounds of spoons against bowls and cups set down on tables, the household dispersed to its tasks. Sister Mercy remained in the kitchen with Sister Hannah to clean the morning's dishes and to begin the midday preparations. Sister Abigail went to the laundry building across the yard, where the week's washing waited in the great tubs. Sister Catherine went to the sewing room on the second floor, where the mending accumulated steadily and required steady attention. A button here, a seam there, the small repairs that kept clothing serviceable. Sister Eunice, who was the youngest of them at thirty-eight, went to the herb garden behind the dwelling to continue the autumn harvest of the medicinal plants that would be dried and stored for winter use.

Ruth herself went to the office.

The office was a small room on the second floor of the main dwelling, with one window facing south and a desk that had been in this room for as long as anyone could remember. The desk was built of cherry wood, its surface dark with age and oil, its drawers organized with the same precision that governed all things here. The desk held ledgers. One for assignments, one for supplies, one for correspondence, one for accounts. And the accumulated paperwork of a community that had always kept careful records because careful records were the memory of the institution, the evidence that things had been done correctly, the proof that could be consulted if proof were ever needed.

Ruth sat in the chair that had been Sister Patience's chair before it was hers, and Sister Clarissa's before that, and she opened the ledger that tracked the daily assignments.

She recorded the morning's attendance at meeting. Seventeen present. Eight women, nine men. Two absent: Sister Mercy in the kitchen, Brother Daniel in the infirmary. She recorded the tasks assigned and the persons assigned to them. She noted Brother Daniel's absence, the reason for it, and the expected duration. She checked the previous week's entries to confirm that the rotation of duties had been maintained correctly. It had.

She reviewed the supply lists, her finger tracing the columns of figures. Flour and sugar were adequate for weeks. Salt had diminished faster than expected—the preserving had required more than she had estimated. It would need replenishment at the trustees' next visit. Candles: the stock held, but the consumption rate had decreased. She noted this without comment in the margin of the ledger. Fewer people required fewer candles. This was arithmetic, not elegy.

The morning passed in this work. The light from the south-facing window moved across the desk, illuminating first the ledger, then the correspondence tray, then the inkwell in its brass holder. Periodically, Ruth rose and walked through the building, checking on the progress of the various tasks, offering a word of guidance here, a question there. The walking was itself a form of work, a necessary survey that confirmed the schedule was holding.

She visited the laundry first. The building was separate from the main dwelling, set back twenty yards across the yard, a practical arrangement that kept the heat and steam away from the living quarters. Inside, Sister Abigail had the work proceeding smoothly. The great copper kettles were steaming, heated by fires built beneath them. The paddles moved in their steady rhythm, agitating the linens in the soapy water. The smell was strong. Lye soap, hot water, and the particular scent of cotton being cleaned. Abigail looked up when Ruth entered, her face flushed from the steam, her sleeves rolled to the elbow.

"The sheets will be done by midday," Abigail said. "The heavier woolens I'll start this afternoon."

Ruth nodded. The schedule was holding.

She returned to the main building and climbed the stairs to the sewing room. Sister Catherine was bent over her work, her needle moving with the same precision it had always shown. The room was bright, lit by windows on two walls, the light falling on the worktable where the mending was spread. Catherine's cough was quieter now. The warmth of the room seemed to ease it. She worked steadily, her fingers finding the rhythm that decades of practice had established.

"The shirts will be finished today," Catherine said without looking up. "The apron that tore, I'll have that done by supper."

Ruth examined the work in progress. The stitches were small and even, nearly invisible against the fabric. Catherine had always been gifted with a needle. Age had not diminished this.

"The thread supply?" Ruth asked.

"Adequate for the month. I'll note what we need for the trustees' list."

Ruth left her to her work and continued her circuit. She checked the kitchen, where the midday meal was taking shape. Soup from yesterday's vegetables, bread from this morning's baking, cheese brought up from the cellar where it aged on its shelves. She checked the herb garden through the window, where Sister Eunice was visible among the plants, her basket filling with the last of the season's harvest.

At midday, the bell rang, and the household gathered for dinner. The meal was simple and sufficient. The men ate on their side, the women on theirs, the silence holding except for the necessary words: please pass, thank you, a murmured request for more bread. Ruth ate without hurry. The soup was well-seasoned, the bread fresh, the cheese sharp and crumbly in the way that indicated proper aging.

After dinner, she returned to the office. There was correspondence to answer. A letter from a trustee regarding the sale of seeds from the summer's garden, another from a former member's family inquiring about records from decades past. Ruth answered both with the brevity that was appropriate, her handwriting small and even, her words chosen for clarity rather than warmth. The letters would go out with the next post. This was enough.

In the middle of the afternoon, Elder Thomas appeared at the office door. Ruth looked up from her work and waited.

"Brother Daniel will need to remain in the infirmary through the week," Elder Thomas said. "The physician came this morning. Rest is required, and time."

Ruth nodded. She had expected this. Brother Daniel was seventy-one, and the illness, while not severe, was slow to release its hold on a body that had less strength to spare than it once had.

"His duties will need covering," she said.

"Yes."

She turned to the ledger where the duty assignments were recorded. Brother Daniel's work was primarily in the woodshop, where he had spent forty years learning the craft and thirty more practicing it. The furniture he made was sold to the outside world through the trustees' arrangements, and the income supported the community's needs. Without him, the shop would need to be staffed by others. Not ideally, but adequately.

"Brother William has some skill," she said, tracing the entries with her finger. "He assisted Brother Daniel last winter, when Daniel's hands were troubling him."

"He did."

"And Brother Joseph can manage the simpler repairs. The chair that came in last week, a loose rung, nothing more. The table leg that needs regluing."

"That would be suitable."

Ruth made the notes in the ledger, the reassignment recorded in the same clear hand as all the other entries. Brother William to the woodshop, mornings. Brother Joseph to assist with repairs, afternoons. Brother Daniel's other duties—the feeding of the chickens, the checking of the fences—were distributed among those who had the capacity to absorb them. The arrangement was not permanent; it would hold until Daniel recovered. The work would be covered. Not as well as Daniel would have covered it—he had spent decades perfecting his craft, and perfection could not be transferred in a week. But adequately.

Elder Thomas watched her write, then nodded once and withdrew. His footsteps receded down the hallway, steady and unhurried. Ruth listened until they faded, then returned to her work.

The afternoon continued. The light moved across the floor of the office, the angle changing as the sun descended toward the hills to the west. Ruth worked through the accounts, through the small administrative tasks that accumulated daily and required daily attention. Each task completed was entered in the ledger. Each task pending was noted for tomorrow. The system recorded itself, creating evidence of its own functioning.

At five o'clock, the bell rang for the evening meeting. The household gathered again in the meeting room, the women on their side, the men on theirs. The light was warmer now, coming from the west, casting longer shadows across the polished floor. Ruth took her usual seat, let her hands rest in her lap, and waited in the silence. Elder Thomas spoke briefly, confirming the reassignments, noting the day's progress. The silence returned, was held, was released.

After supper, soup again, the last of the bread, stewed apples from the cellar stores, there was an hour of rest before the final bell. Ruth used this time as she always did: to complete the day's administrative tasks, to close the ledgers, to prepare the next day's assignments.

She stood at the slate board in the hallway, chalk in hand, writing the names and tasks in her careful script. Sister Mercy: kitchen, morning. Sister Hannah: kitchen, afternoon. Sister Abigail: laundry. Sister Catherine: sewing. Sister Eunice: garden, then preserving shed. The names filled the spaces on the board. The tasks aligned with the names. There were no gaps, no overlaps, no uncertainties. Each person had work. Each work had a person.

She stepped back and looked at the board. The arrangement was complete. A precise fit. If Sister Catherine's cough worsened and she could not work, the sewing would fall behind. If Brother William proved less capable in the woodshop than expected, the repairs would accumulate. If the weather turned early, the garden work would need to accelerate. The system held, but it held by exact fit, not by abundance. There was no margin.

Ruth set down the chalk and dusted her hands on her apron. The board was ready for tomorrow. The ledger was closed. The correspondence was answered. The day was complete.

The final bell rang at eight o'clock. The household gathered for evening prayers, the familiar words spoken and received, the quiet voices mingling in the dim room. Then the dispersal, the climbing of stairs, the closing of doors. Ruth undressed in the sequence that reversed the morning's sequence, knelt in private prayer, and climbed into bed.

The sheets were cool at first, then warmed. The room was dark. Sister Abigail's breathing slowed and deepened into sleep. Outside, an owl called. Once, twice. Then fell silent.

Ruth lay in the darkness. She thought about the ledger page. The names in their columns. The tasks in their rows. She thought about the supply lists and the requests she would make when the trustees came. She thought about the empty rooms, the extra place settings, and the candle consumption that had decreased.

She thought about the precise fit. The system that held.

Tomorrow she would make another arrangement, and it would be correct for that day's circumstances. This was her work. This was what the system required.

The house was quiet. The village was still. The night held everything in its proper place.

In the quiet, just before sleep took her, Ruth heard it again. The hum. That low sustained note, as if the building remembered holding something it no longer held. As if the walls had learned a frequency long ago and could not quite forget it.

She listened.

The hum faded, or she stopped hearing it, or sleep arrived and carried her past the place where such things could be noticed.

The system slept.

And she slept with it.

CHAPTER THREE

Roles

Sister Eunice had been in the herb garden since first light, earlier than her assignment required. Ruth saw her from the office window during the hour before the morning bell. A figure moving among the rows, bending and rising, bending and rising, the rhythm of her work visible even at a distance. The basket beside her was already half full by the time the bell rang, and when the household gathered for meeting, Eunice's hands still carried the green smell of the plants she had been harvesting. The smell was visible in the meeting room, in the way the sisters on either side of Eunice glanced at her hands, in the way the smell entered the silence and became part of it.

Ruth noticed this. She noticed most things. It was her function to notice, to observe the small variations in routine that might signal a need for adjustment. The function had a name now, a practical name: oversight, administration, the keeping of order. But once it had been called something else. Ruth did not think of this, had not thought of it in years. But somewhere in the practice of noticing, in the discipline of attending to where attention was needed, there was an older practice. Watching for the gift. Observing where the spirit moved next. The watching had become watching. The gift had become routine. But the attention itself remained, passed down through generations of women who sat in this seat and kept this ledger and noticed what needed to be noticed.

Eunice had been arriving early for three weeks now, perhaps four. The early arrivals were not against any rule. There was no rule against beginning work before the assigned hour. But they were unusual. Eunice had always been punctual, precise, her labor matching exactly the schedule Ruth had written on the board. This new pattern was something else. Initiative, perhaps. Or something that looked like initiative but was not.

Ruth had asked her two weeks ago why she came early. Eunice had not been able to explain it clearly. She woke before the bell, she said. Her body woke. She lay in the dark waiting for sleep to return, but sleep did not return. Her hands wanted to move. Her legs wanted to carry her somewhere. The garden was where she went because the garden was where her work was, and the work steadied her, gave the restlessness somewhere to go.

Ruth had listened and said nothing. But she had recognized something in the description. The body trained, over generations, to move toward labor as worship. The body that did not distinguish between the bell's call and its own need. The training had outlasted the reasoning. The discipline remained after the understanding had faded. Eunice's body woke early because bodies here had always woken early, had always moved toward work as toward prayer, had always found in labor the stillness that others found in rest. She did not know why she could not sleep. She only knew that the garden called her, and she went.

After the morning meeting, Ruth went to the herb garden herself. The day was cool, the sky a flat gray that promised neither rain nor clearing, the kind of sky that would hold until evening without changing. The path to the garden was well-worn, packed earth that had been walked for decades, the grass on either side trimmed back each spring to keep the edges clean. The garden itself was set behind the main dwelling, sheltered from the north wind by a stone wall, positioned to catch the morning and afternoon sun.

It was a good location. The location had been chosen by Sister Abigail Whitmore in 1798, according to the records Ruth had once consulted when questions arose about the garden's history. Sister Abigail had known where things should go. She had the gift for it, the records said. The gift had come to her in meeting, in the years when gifts still came. She had stood in the open field behind the dwelling, the records said, and she had felt where the herbs wanted to be planted. The feeling had moved through her like certainty, and she had marked the ground, and the garden had been built where she marked it. The herbs had thrived. They still thrived, a hundred years later, in the place a woman had chosen because something moved through her and told her this was right.

Ruth did not think about Sister Abigail Whitmore as she walked the path. She thought about the schedule, about the assignments, about the question Eunice had raised, and the answer that did not exist. But the garden was where it was because someone had once stood in a field and felt something. The garden continued because the feeling had been correct. The feeling was gone now, or no longer spoken of, but the garden remained.

Eunice was already back at work, her knees on the canvas pad she used to protect her dress from the damp earth, her hands moving among the sage plants with the careful motion of someone who had been taught what she was doing and had practiced it until the teaching became unnecessary. Her posture was efficient, her movements economical. No wasted effort, no hesitation. She had learned this work well.

Ruth watched from the edge of the garden, not yet announcing herself. The motion of Eunice's hands had a rhythm. Reach, cut, place. Reach, cut, place. The rhythm was steady, almost hypnotic. And the larger motion, the bending and rising, bending and rising, had a rhythm too. Ruth watched it without quite seeing it, the way one watches a familiar thing without registering what makes it familiar.

Then she saw it.

The bending and rising. The steady pulse of it. If someone were watching from a distance, not knowing what the motion meant, not knowing it was harvesting, the rhythm might look like something else. Like the body reaching for a movement it no longer makes. Like the echo of a different kind of rising and falling, a different kind of work the body once knew and had been trained to forget. Eunice did not think about the rhythm. She was thinking about sage, about the yellowing leaves, about the frost that would come. But her body moved in the old way, the way bodies here had always moved, bending and rising, bending and rising, as if the work and the worship had never been separated, as if the hands harvesting herbs were the same hands that had once reached toward something else entirely.

Ruth blinked. The moment passed. Eunice was simply harvesting sage, nothing more.

"The sage is ready," Eunice said without looking up. She knew Ruth's footsteps, could distinguish them from the footsteps of the other sisters. This knowledge had come without intention, simply from years of hearing the same sounds in the same sequences, the mind cataloging what the ears received. "Another day and it would have been too late. The leaves were starting to yellow at the edges."

Ruth looked at the plants. The sage had indeed been ready. Eunice's assessment was correct. The harvested stems were properly trimmed, the leaves intact, the cut ends clean. Good work. Competent work. There was nothing to correct.

"You've been starting early," Ruth said.

It was not a question, but it invited a response. Eunice's hands paused for a moment, then continued their work. She pulled a stem, examined it, added it to the basket. The basket was nearly full now, the sage packed loosely to allow air circulation, arranged in the way that would make the transfer to the drying racks easier.

"There's more to do," she said. "The thyme needs cutting before the frost. The chamomile should have been dried a week ago. The lavender." She stopped herself, shook her head slightly. "There's more to do than the hours allow."

Ruth considered this. It was true that the herb garden had grown larger over the years, that the medicinal preparations the community produced for sale had become more varied and more numerous. The preparations were important. They brought income, they served the sick in the surrounding towns, they represented skill that had been accumulated over generations. It was also true that Eunice was the only one now who worked the garden regularly. Sister Margaret, who had taught Eunice the craft, had passed four winters ago. Sister Anne, who had assisted, had left the community the year before that. Not in anger or doubt, but simply because she had felt called to return to the world, a calling the elders had accepted without argument because such callings, though rare, were not forbidden.

Now there was only Eunice. And the garden was the same size it had always been. The rows had not shortened. The beds had not narrowed. The work remained what it had always been; only the hands had changed.

"The schedule can be adjusted," Ruth said. "If more time is needed."

"More time from where?" Eunice's voice was not sharp, but it was direct in a way that approached sharpness. She looked up now, her eyes meeting Ruth's briefly before returning to the plants. Her eyes were tired, Ruth noticed. Not the tiredness of a single night's poor sleep, but the accumulated tiredness of weeks, months, of rising before the bell and working after supper and still not finishing what needed to be finished. "Everyone has their work. The kitchen needs Hannah and Mercy. The laundry needs Abigail. Catherine's hands are the only ones that can do the fine mending. Where would the extra hours come from?"

It was a reasonable question, asked reasonably. Ruth did not have an immediate answer, because there was no immediate answer. The schedule was what it was. The people were who they were. The work required what it required.

"I'll review the assignments," Ruth said. "There may be adjustments possible."

Eunice nodded, but the nod was not agreement. It was acknowledgment. The acknowledgment of someone who had heard what was said and did not expect it to change anything. She returned to her work, and after a moment, Ruth left her there, walking back toward the main dwelling with the problem turning in her mind.

The problem was not the garden. The problem was not even the schedule, not exactly. The problem was the nature of roles themselves, the way they accumulated over time, the way a person who was competent at one thing became, by that competence, responsible for all of it. Eunice had been assigned to the herb garden eight years ago, when she was thirty. She had learned the plants, the timing, the methods of drying and preparing. She had learned well, and her learning had been rewarded with more responsibility. The reward was not intended as a burden. It was intended as trust, as recognition, as the acknowledgment that she had become what the role required. But trust and burden were sometimes difficult to distinguish. The weight of the one felt very much like the weight of the other.

Ruth returned to the office and opened the assignment ledger. She turned back through the pages, month by month, looking at the names and the tasks, looking for the pattern she already knew was there. Eight years ago, the herb garden had been staffed by three sisters. Five years ago, two. Now, one. The numbers were clear, written in her own hand and the hands of those who had kept the ledger before her. The garden had not shrunk. The work had not diminished. Only the hands had.

She made a note in the margin, a small mark that meant "review." Then she closed the ledger and continued with the day's work.

The morning passed in its usual rhythm. Ruth checked the kitchen first, where Sister Mercy was directing the preparation of the midday meal with the same quiet efficiency she had directed it for thirty-one years. Mercy's hands were slower now than they had been. Ruth had noticed this over the past year. The slight hesitation before lifting a heavy pot, the way she rested her palms on the work table when she thought no one was watching, the delegation of tasks that required bending or reaching to Sister Hannah, who was younger and whose back did not ache when the weather changed. But Mercy's judgment was unchanged. She knew what needed to be done and in what order, and she communicated this to Hannah with the minimum of words necessary.

Hannah was learning. She was not naturally suited to kitchen work. Her instincts were toward order and arrangement, the setting of tables, the alignment of objects in precise rows. But she was learning because the kitchen needed her, and there was no one else to learn. She would never have Mercy's feel for seasoning, for the moment when bread was ready to come out of the oven, for the temperature of oil that meant it was time to add the vegetables. But she would learn enough. Enough was what the system required.

"The bread rose well," Mercy said when Ruth entered. "Better than yesterday. Hannah is improving."

Hannah looked up from the vegetables she was chopping, her face flushing slightly at the praise. The flush was pride, Ruth recognized, the particular pride of someone who had accomplished something difficult. But there was something else in it too. A recognition that the praise was also assessment, that her improvement was being measured against a standard she had not yet reached and might never fully reach.

"The soup will be ready by the bell," Mercy continued. "The stores are holding. We'll need more onions from the root cellar tomorrow, and the dried beans are lower than I'd like. I've noted it for your list."

Ruth nodded and made the note in her ledger. The kitchen was functioning. Mercy was functioning. Hannah was learning.

She continued her rounds. The laundry building was next, set back twenty yards across the yard. Sister Abigail had the work proceeding smoothly, the great copper kettles steaming, the paddles moving in their steady rhythm. Abigail was forty-six, strong in body if not in conversation. She spoke rarely and worked constantly, her hands always occupied with some task, her mind apparently content with the repetition of lifting and stirring and wringing. Ruth had known her for twenty-three years and could not have said what Abigail thought about anything other than laundry. Perhaps she thought about nothing else. Perhaps the work had become so complete in her that there was no space left for other thoughts.

"The sheets will be done by midday," Abigail said, the words the same words she said every week when Ruth came to check. "The heavier woolens this afternoon."

Ruth nodded and noted the progress. The laundry was functioning. Abigail was functioning. The work continued.

She returned to the main building and climbed the stairs to the sewing room. Sister Catherine was at her usual place by the window, her needle moving through fabric with the precision that decades of practice had given her. The cough was present. It was always present now. But it was quiet today, more a clearing of the throat than the deep spasms that sometimes interrupted her work.

"The mending is nearly finished," Catherine said. "Brother Joseph's coat needed more work than I expected. The seams were worn through in three places. He doesn't notice these things. Men don't."

"No," Ruth agreed. "They don't."

She sat down across from Catherine, not to work, she had her own tasks waiting, but to be present for a moment. Catherine was the oldest of the sisters now, eighty-two in the spring, and her presence in the sewing room was more than functional. She was the memory of how things had been done, the repository of techniques and standards that could not be written in any ledger. When she was gone, something would be lost that could not be replaced. Not the stitches themselves, which could be taught, but the judgment behind them, the knowledge of when a garment could be mended and when it must be retired, the feel for fabric that came only from handling it for sixty years.

"Eunice came to see me yesterday," Catherine said, her needle not pausing. The needle was bone, old and yellowed, worn smooth by her grip. She had used the same needle for as long as Ruth could remember. "She asked if I could teach her the finer stitches. The ones for the sale goods."

Ruth waited. Catherine would continue when she was ready.

"I told her I would try. But my eyes." Catherine shook her head slightly, the motion careful, as if she were conserving even that small expenditure of energy. "The close work is harder now. I can do it, but I cannot teach it. Teaching requires seeing what the student does wrong, and I cannot always see that anymore. The light isn't what it was. Or my eyes aren't what they were. The result is the same."

"Perhaps in good light," Ruth said. "The south window."

"Perhaps." Catherine's tone suggested she did not believe this, but would not argue. Arguments required energy she no longer had in abundance. "She's capable, Eunice. Quick with her hands, quick with her mind. But the garden takes all her time. She has no hours left for learning something new. She comes to me in the evenings, after supper, and I see how tired she is. The learning doesn't go in when the body is that tired."

Ruth heard what Catherine was saying, and what she was not saying. Eunice was stretched. The work was expanding while the hands diminished.

"I'll speak with Elder Thomas," Ruth said. "There may be adjustments possible."

She said this knowing that the adjustments, if they came, would be small. But the saying of it mattered, the acknowledgment that the problem had been heard and would be considered. That was part of her role too. The receiving of concerns, the translation of individual strain into institutional language, the assurance that the system was aware of what it asked.

She returned to the office and wrote a note for Elder Thomas, brief and factual. Sister Eunice requests additional time for the herb garden. The current assignment may be insufficient for the work required. She suggested a review of the labor distribution, not as criticism but as maintenance, the routine checking of a mechanism to ensure it continued to function smoothly.

The note would be delivered. It would be read. It would be considered. What happened after that was not hers to determine.

The afternoon brought a visitor to the village. Not a common occurrence, but not rare either. A woman from the town, middle-aged, her dress plain but of good quality, her manner respectful but direct. She had come to inquire about a piece of furniture, a writing desk her father had ordered before his death. The order had been placed with Brother Daniel, who was still in the infirmary, and the woman did not know whether the work had been completed.

Ruth met her at the entrance to the office building, as was proper. Visitors were received formally, and their business conducted in the spaces designated for such purposes. The woman introduced herself. Mrs. Ashworth, her father had been Mr. Pelham, the desk was to have been cherry wood with brass fittings, ordered in the spring. Ruth listened, then consulted the ledger where such orders were recorded.

"The desk was completed in August," Ruth said. "It is in the workshop, awaiting delivery. Brother Daniel noted that the delivery was to wait until the roads improved after the autumn rains."

Mrs. Ashworth nodded. "The roads are better now. My father passed in September. He never saw it finished. Could I see it? He spoke of it often before he passed. He was particular about furniture."

Ruth considered. It was not usual for visitors to enter the workshop, but it was not forbidden. The desk belonged to Mrs. Ashworth now, or would once payment was received. There was no reason to refuse.

She led the woman across the yard to the workshop, a long building set apart from the dwellings, its doors wide enough to admit the large pieces of furniture that were sometimes commissioned. Inside, the air smelled of sawdust and varnish and the particular sweetness of cherry wood that had been cut and shaped and finished. Brother William was at one of the benches, working on a simple chair, his movements careful but not confident. He had the stance of someone following instructions rather than following instinct. He looked up when they entered, nodded once to Ruth, and returned to his work without speaking.

The desk was in the corner, covered with a cloth to protect it from dust. Ruth removed the cloth and stepped back so Mrs. Ashworth could see.

The desk was beautiful. Ruth recognized this, though beauty was not a quality she often had occasion to consider. The wood glowed in the afternoon light, the grain visible beneath the finish, the brass fittings bright against the dark cherry. The proportions were exact, balanced, pleasing in a way that required no explanation. The drawers moved smoothly when Mrs. Ashworth tested them, sliding open and closed without sound. It was the work of someone who had spent seventy years learning how wood behaved and what could be asked of it.

Mrs. Ashworth ran her hand along the edge of the desk, her touch careful, almost reverent. Her eyes were bright with something that might have been grief or might have been recognition. "He would have loved this," she said quietly. "My father. He would have loved it."

Ruth said nothing. There was nothing to say. The desk spoke for itself, for the hands that had made it, for the decades of skill that had gone into every joint and surface.

"Brother Daniel made this?" Mrs. Ashworth asked.

"Yes."

"Is he well? I heard he was ill."

"He is recovering. Rest is required."

Mrs. Ashworth looked around the workshop, at Brother William bent over his simple chair, at the tools arranged on their pegs along the wall, at the wood stacked and waiting to be used. Her gaze returned to the desk, to the quality of its making. "Will there be someone to continue his work? When he can no longer." She stopped, perhaps recognizing that she had asked something too direct, too close to the questions that polite visitors did not ask.

"There will be someone," Ruth said. It was the correct answer, the answer the system required her to give. Whether it was true was a different question, one she did not allow herself to consider.

The arrangements were made. The desk would be delivered the following week, when Brother William could be spared to drive the wagon. Payment was received. Mrs. Ashworth had brought it with her, perhaps expecting this outcome. The amount was recorded in the ledger. The visitor departed, her carriage rattling down the lane toward the main road, the sound diminishing until it was absorbed by the larger silence of the valley.

Ruth stood in the yard after the carriage had gone, looking at the buildings that surrounded her. The main dwelling. The workshop. The laundry. The barns. Each building had been constructed for a purpose, and each purpose was still served. The buildings did not know that fewer hands maintained them now, that fewer feet walked their halls. They simply stood, as they had stood for a hundred years, waiting to be used.

At the evening meeting, Elder Thomas spoke briefly about the visitor, about the completed order, and about the income it represented. He spoke of Brother Daniel's continued recovery and of the work Brother William was doing in his absence. He spoke of the day's progress. The laundry completed, the mending current, the kitchen well-stocked. He did not speak of the future. The future was not his concern; the present was.

After the meeting, Ruth found a moment to give him her note about Sister Eunice. He read it, his face showing nothing, his expression the same patient attention he gave to all matters brought before him. He nodded once.

"I will consider it," he said. "Perhaps there are adjustments possible."

Ruth accepted his response as she had offered her own: as a necessary part of the process, a form to be observed even when the content was uncertain.

Supper was quiet. The household ate in the usual silence, the usual passing of dishes, the usual small sounds of consumption. Ruth watched. She was always watching. And she saw what she always saw: people performing their roles, the system operating, the day nearing its end.

After supper, she made her rounds. The kitchen was clean, the dishes washed and stored, the morning's preparations begun. The fires were banked. The doors were secured. The animals were fed and sheltered for the night. Each task completed, each role performed, each person in their place.

She stopped at the herb garden on her way back to the dwelling. Eunice was not there. She would be in the preserving shed, drying the day's harvest. But the garden itself was visible in the last light, the rows neat, the plants tended, the work evident in every trimmed stem and weeded path.

The garden was too large for one person. This was simply true. It had been planted for three, maintained by two, and was now tended by one.

Ruth turned and walked to the preserving shed. Eunice was inside, arranging the sage stems on the drying racks, her movements efficient but slower than they had been that morning. Fatigue showed in the set of her shoulders, in the careful way she placed each stem as if her hands needed to think about what they were doing.

"The sage is drying well," Ruth said from the doorway.

Eunice nodded without turning. "It should be ready in three days. The chamomile will take longer. A week, perhaps more. The lavender is nearly done."

Ruth stepped into the shed. The air was warm and fragrant, thick with the smell of drying herbs. The racks lined the walls, each one labeled in Eunice's careful hand, each one filled with the summer's harvest being preserved against the winter's need.

"I've spoken with Elder Thomas," Ruth said. "About the schedule."

Eunice's hands paused. "And?"

"He will consider it."

The words hung in the warm air. Eunice resumed her work, placing the last of the sage stems on the rack, adjusting their position so the air could circulate properly.

"I know what that means," she said quietly. "It means nothing will change. It means I'll keep doing what I'm doing until I can't do it anymore, and then someone else will be assigned, and they'll learn what I know, and the garden will continue."

Ruth did not correct her. There was nothing to correct.

"The garden is important," Eunice continued. "The medicines we make, the sales to the towns. I understand why it matters. I'm not asking to be relieved. I'm asking for." She stopped, shook her head. "I don't know what I'm asking for. Time that doesn't exist. Hands that aren't here. A different way of doing what has to be done."

Ruth watched her finish the work, straighten the racks, brush the dried leaves from her apron. Eunice was thirty-eight years old, strong and capable, skilled at work she had not chosen but had accepted because acceptance was what the system required.

"The schedule for tomorrow is the same," Ruth said. "But I've noted you for lighter duties in the afternoon. The preserving can wait one more day. The garden cannot."

It was a small adjustment, the only adjustment she had the authority to make. A few hours shifted, a task deferred, a small space opened in the relentless accumulation of work. Eunice looked at her, and for a moment something passed between them. An acknowledgment, perhaps, of what had been asked and what had been given and the distance between them.

"Thank you," Eunice said.

Ruth nodded and left the shed. The evening was full dark now, the stars appearing one by one in the clear sky.

She walked toward the dwelling, then paused at the edge of the herb garden. The rows were dark, the plants invisible except as shapes against the soil. The air was cold and carried the faint scent of sage.

The garden waited. It would wait through the night, through the frost, through whatever came. In the morning, someone would return to it.

The slate board would be waiting in the hallway, blank for a few hours yet.

Ruth turned and walked inside.

CHAPTER FOUR

Confession

The confession meetings were held on the first and third Thursdays of each month, in the small room off the main meeting hall that had been built for this purpose. The room was plain even by the standards of plainness that governed all things here. White walls, a single window facing north, two chairs placed at an angle that allowed conversation without direct confrontation. The chairs were identical, built of maple, their seats worn smooth by decades of sitting. There was nothing else in the room. Nothing to distract. Nothing to soften.

Ruth arrived early, as she always did when she was assigned to witness. The room was empty, the morning light thin and gray through the north-facing window. She stood in the doorway for a moment, letting her eyes adjust, and then she saw it.

The floor.

She had seen it before. She saw it every time she came to this room. But this morning, in this particular light, the wear was visible in a way it was not always visible. A circle. Faint, almost erased by the years of feet walking in straight lines to and from the chairs. But present, if you knew to look. The boards were worn in a curve, a pattern that had nothing to do with sitting or standing or the kind of walking that happened now. The circle was perhaps eight feet across, centered in the room, its edges soft and uncertain, but its shape unmistakable once you saw it.

Ruth looked at it. She did not think about what had made it. She simply looked, and then she walked to the window and opened it slightly, just enough to let the autumn air move through the room, and she did not look at the floor again.

The witnessing was part of her role now, had been for the past seven years. Witnessing was not judgment; it was presence. The elders heard confession and offered guidance, but someone must sit beside the confessor; someone must be the proof that words spoken in private were also spoken in community.

The morning was cool, the air smelled of damp earth and fallen leaves, the particular smell of late October when the growing season was finished and the preserving was done and the community turned inward toward the long work of winter.

Elder Thomas arrived at the appointed hour. He carried nothing. The record was kept elsewhere, in the ledger Ruth maintained, where confessions were noted not by content but by occurrence. Sister Abigail, October 17, 1897. The names and dates, nothing more.

"Sister Eunice will come first," Elder Thomas said, taking his seat. "Then, Sister Hannah. Sister Catherine has asked to be excused. Her cough is worse this morning."

Ruth took her own seat, the witnessing chair, positioned to the side where she could see both the confessor's face and Elder Thomas's. The chair was uncomfortable by design. Witnessing required alertness. The body must stay present even when the words became routine.

Eunice entered at the appointed time. She had washed her hands. Ruth could see the dampness on her skin, the care she had taken to come clean. Her dress was neat, her cap properly tied, her manner composed. She did not look at Ruth. This was proper. The witness was present but not addressed.

She sat in the confessor's chair and folded her hands in her lap. Her hands were red from the work in the garden, the skin roughened by soil and stems, the nails trimmed short and scrubbed clean. Working hands. Capable hands. Hands that had been moving since first light and would continue moving until the evening bell.

"I am ready," she said.

Elder Thomas nodded. His face was patient, attentive, without expectation. This was how he always looked during confession. Present without pressure, receptive without eagerness.

"Speak what you have to speak," he said. The words were the same words that began every confession, had begun every confession for as long as anyone could remember. The formula was part of the practice. It created the space.

Eunice was silent for a moment. Her eyes were fixed on a point beyond Elder Thomas's shoulder, the white wall behind him, the nothing that was there. Ruth watched her face, the small movements of thought visible in the set of her mouth, the slight tension around her eyes.

"I have felt resentment," Eunice said. Her voice was steady, neither loud nor soft, pitched to be heard by the two people in the room and no further. "About the garden. About the hours. I have risen before the bell and worked after supper, and still the work is not finished, and I have felt that this is unfair. That I am asked to do what cannot be done. That the failure is not mine but the system's."

She paused. Ruth kept her face neutral, her body still. This was not new. She had heard Eunice speak of this before, in different words, with different emphasis, but the substance was familiar. The garden was too large. The hands were too few. The strain was real.

"I have spoken of this to Sister Ruth," Eunice continued, "and she has spoken to you, and you have said you will consider adjustments. I confess that I did not believe you. I confess that I thought the words were only words, spoken to satisfy me, not to change anything. I confess that I have carried this doubt and let it harden into something like contempt."

Ruth felt the words land, felt the small shock of being named in confession, of hearing her own role reflected back in Eunice's voice. She had known that Eunice doubted. She had seen it in the nod that was not agreement, in the tired eyes, in the careful way Eunice had received the promise of consideration. But hearing it spoken was different. Speech made it real in a way that knowledge did not.

Elder Thomas received this without visible reaction. His face remained patient, his posture unchanged. Contempt was not a small thing. It was a failure of charity, a hardening of the heart against the community that had given one a place and a purpose. But his manner did not shift to match the seriousness of the word. All confessions were received the same way. The gravity was in the speaking, not in the hearing.

"I confess also," Eunice said, "that I have envied Sister Hannah. She works in the kitchen, where the work ends when the meal is served, where the hours are bounded, where there is help. I have watched her in the evenings, sitting in the common room with her mending, and I have wished that my work could end the way hers ends. I have wished that I could be finished."

Her voice caught slightly on the last word. Not a break, not tears, but a tightness that revealed how close the feeling was to the surface. Ruth watched and did not move. This was part of witnessing too. The observation of what confession cost, the recognition that speaking was not easy, even when speaking was required.

"I have tried to release this envy," Eunice continued. "I have prayed for Sister Hannah's happiness without comparing it to my own. But the envy returns. It returns when I am tired. It returns when the work exceeds the hours. I confess that I have not succeeded in removing it."

She fell silent. But the silence was not complete. Ruth watched Eunice's face and saw something else there. A gathering. A pressure behind the eyes. Eunice's mouth opened slightly, as if another word wanted to come out. Something that was not resentment, not envy, not any of the tokens she had offered. Something older. Something that did not have a name, or had a name she did not know, or had a name that was no longer spoken.

The pause lasted two breaths. Ruth counted them. Eunice's mouth stayed open, the word or the sound or whatever it was pressing against the inside of her lips.

Then it passed. Eunice closed her mouth. She swallowed. When she spoke again, her voice was steady, the moment gone as if it had never been.

"That is all," she said.

But Ruth was no longer entirely in the room.

The pause, the almost-speaking, the pressure that had not found release. It had reminded her of something. Something she had not thought of in years, had not had reason to think of, had perhaps chosen not to think of because thinking of it served no purpose.

Sister Clarissa. Twenty years ago. This same room.

Ruth had been new to witnessing then, still learning the posture, the silence, the particular quality of attention the role required. Elder Patience had been in the chair where Elder Thomas sat now. Clarissa had been in the confessor's chair, her hands folded the way Eunice's hands were folded, her voice steady as she began.

The confession had started as confessions started. Words, carefully chosen, describing failures of patience or charity or attention. Ruth could not remember the specifics now. They had been ordinary. They had been tokens, the kind of tokens Eunice had just offered, the kind of tokens everyone offered because confession required offering, and the offering had to take some form.

But then something had changed.

Clarissa had paused. The same kind of pause Eunice had just made. Mouth open, pressure building, a sense that something else wanted to come out. But where Eunice had closed her mouth and swallowed and continued, Clarissa had not.

Clarissa had stopped speaking. Her hands, folded in her lap, had begun to tremble. The trembling had started small, barely visible, a vibration in the fingers. Then it had moved up her arms, into her shoulders, into her whole frame. She was shaking. Not violently, not with convulsion, but with a steady tremor that seemed to come from somewhere deeper than muscle, somewhere the body did not usually access.

Elder Patience had risen from his chair.

Ruth remembered this clearly now, the image sharp after twenty years of forgetting. Elder Patience had risen. He had crossed the small space between his chair and Clarissa's. He had placed his hands on her shoulders.

The touch had been firm. Ruth remembered that too. Not tentative, not questioning. Firm, as if Elder Patience knew exactly what was happening and exactly what was required. His hands on her shoulders, his weight steady, his presence holding her as the tremor moved through her.

And then something had happened that Ruth had never seen before and had never seen since.

The shaking had passed out of Clarissa. Not stopped. Passed. It had moved through Elder Patience's hands and into his arms and through his body, and then, somehow, it had been in the room itself. Ruth had felt it. She had felt the weight of whatever Clarissa was carrying pass through the elder and into the air, into the walls, into the community that was present in the form of Ruth's witnessing.

The room had held it. The room had absorbed it. The weight had gone somewhere, and the somewhere was not Clarissa anymore.

When it ended, Clarissa was weeping. Not the quiet tears of ordinary grief, but the deep weeping of someone who had been emptied, who had released something she had carried so long she had forgotten she was carrying it.

"Thank you," she had said. Her voice had been hoarse, barely audible. "It needed to go somewhere."

Elder Patience had returned to his chair. His face had been calm, unsurprised, as if what had just happened was not extraordinary but simply part of what confession could be, what confession was meant to be, when the need was great enough, and the willingness was complete.

Ruth had never spoken of it. She had never asked Elder Patience what had happened or what it meant. She had never heard anyone else speak of it. Clarissa had died three years later, quietly, in her sleep, and whatever she had released in that room had gone with her into whatever came after.

Ruth had forgotten. She had not chosen to forget. The memory had simply receded, covered over by the years of ordinary confessions, the tokens exchanged and received, the friction removed, and the smooth functioning restored. There had been no reason to remember. The practice continued. The form was maintained. What use was a memory of something that no longer happened?

But now, watching Eunice's mouth close on the word she did not speak, Ruth remembered.

"Sister Ruth."

Elder Thomas's voice. Ruth blinked. The room came back into focus. Eunice was gone. When had Eunice left? Ruth had missed it. She had been somewhere else, twenty years away, and she had missed Eunice's departure.

"Sister Hannah is waiting," Elder Thomas said. His tone was patient, but there was a question in it. A noticing. He had seen her absence, her distance, the moment when she had stopped witnessing and started remembering.

"Yes," Ruth said. "Of course."

She straightened in her chair. The chair was uncomfortable. The discomfort was intentional. It was meant to keep her present, alert, attending to what was spoken in this room. She had failed at that, for a moment. She would not fail again.

Sister Hannah entered.

Hannah was younger than Eunice by fifteen years, new to the community by relative measure. She had been here only twelve years, had come as a young woman of twenty-three when her family could no longer support her, and the world outside had offered nothing she wanted. She was still learning what confession required, still finding the language for what she carried.

She sat in the confessor's chair with her hands clasped tight, her knuckles white. Her face was pale, her eyes fixed on the floor. Ruth recognized this posture. Hannah was afraid. Not of Elder Thomas, not of the practice itself, but of the speaking. Some people feared silence. Hannah feared words.

"Speak what you have to speak," Elder Thomas said, the formula unchanged.

Hannah swallowed. Her throat moved visibly. She opened her mouth, closed it, opened it again.

"I have had thoughts," she said. Her voice was barely audible. Ruth leaned slightly forward, not to hear better, she could hear, but to convey attention, to let Hannah feel that her words, however quiet, were being received.

"Thoughts about leaving," Hannah continued. "About the world outside. About what my life would be if I had not come here. I know these thoughts are wrong. I know I chose this life and the choice was right. But the thoughts come anyway, especially at night, especially when I am tired."

She stopped. Her hands twisted in her lap, the fingers interlacing and releasing and interlacing again. Ruth watched and said nothing. Watching was her role. Silence was her role. The words were Hannah's to find.

"I confess that I do not always feel grateful," Hannah said. "The kitchen work is good work. Sister Mercy is patient with me. The food we make feeds people who need feeding. But sometimes I stand at the stove and I think: this is all there will ever be. This stove. This pot. This steam. Every day until I die."

Her voice had steadied as she spoke, gaining strength from the speaking itself. This was common. The first words were the hardest. Once they were out, the rest followed more easily.

"I confess that I have imagined other lives," she continued. "A husband. Children. A house of my own. I know that these imaginings are contrary to the life I chose, contrary to the beliefs I hold. Celibacy is not deprivation; it is devotion. I know this. I believe this. But the imaginings come anyway, and I have not been able to stop them."

Elder Thomas listened. His face showed nothing but attention. He sat in his chair, his posture unchanged, his hands resting on his knees. He did not rise. He did not reach toward Hannah. He received her words as words were received now: with patience, with attention, with the assurance that speaking was enough, that the speaking itself accomplished what needed to be accomplished.

Ruth watched him and thought of Elder Patience rising. The hands on Clarissa's shoulders. The weight passing through.

"Is there more?" Elder Thomas asked when Hannah fell silent.

Hannah hesitated. Ruth saw something flicker across her face. A thought held back, a word not spoken. But the flicker passed, and Hannah shook her head.

"No," she said. "That is all."

"Then you are heard," Elder Thomas said. "The thoughts you describe are not sin. They are the mind's wandering, the imagination's restlessness. You have spoken them, and in speaking them you have released their power. They cannot harm you now. You may return to your work, and when the thoughts return, as they may, you may bring them here again, and they will be received again, as many times as necessary."

Hannah rose. Her face was calmer now, the fear replaced by something like relief. She nodded once to Elder Thomas, did not look at Ruth, and left the room.

Ruth noted the time. Hannah, October 17, 1897.

The morning continued. Sister Mercy came, and her confession was brief and practical. She had been sharp with Hannah twice this week, had spoken more curtly than charity required, had allowed her frustration with aging hands to become frustration with the young hands that could not yet do what hers once did. She spoke without drama, received Elder Thomas's acknowledgment without visible emotion, and returned to the kitchen where the midday meal was waiting to be prepared.

Sister Abigail came. Her confession was the shortest Ruth had witnessed in years. She had neglected her evening prayers twice, falling asleep before she could complete them. She had felt no particular remorse about this, only the vague sense that the omission should be spoken. Elder Thomas received this with the same patience he had shown the others, offered the same formula of release, and Abigail departed as silently as she had arrived.

By midday, the women's confessions were complete. The room was quiet now, empty except for Ruth and Elder Thomas, the two chairs returned to their positions, the window still open to the cool air that had grown colder as the morning progressed.

"Sister Catherine will need to be seen next week," Elder Thomas said. "Her cough concerns me. The physician should be called if it does not improve."

Ruth nodded. "I will note it for the schedule."

"The confessions were ordinary," Elder Thomas continued. He was not speaking to her exactly. More thinking aloud, the way he sometimes did after confession, processing what he had heard. "Sister Eunice's resentment is known and has been known. We have discussed adjustments. They will be made when they can be made. Until then, she will continue as she has continued, and the confession will allow her to continue without the weight of carrying what she has now spoken."

Ruth said nothing. This was not a conversation; it was a summary. Her role was to receive it, not to respond.

"Sister Hannah's imaginings are the imaginings of youth," Elder Thomas continued. "They will fade as she settles more fully into the life she has chosen."

He rose from his chair, slowly, the care of age visible in the way he steadied himself, the way his hand found the chair's arm before he trusted his legs to hold him. He was seventy-four now. Ruth remembered when he had been vigorous, when his movements had been quick and certain. The slowing had come gradually, so gradually that she had not noticed it until it was complete.

"The practice is good," he said. "It has always been good. When confession is regular, when nothing accumulates, when every strain is spoken as it arises, the community remains healthy. The friction is removed before it can become damage. This is what the founders understood. This is what we maintain."

He walked to the door, paused, turned back.

"You witness well, Sister Ruth. You have always witnessed well. The watching without judgment, the presence without intrusion. These are difficult, and you do them with grace."

Ruth accepted the praise as she accepted all praise. With a nod, without elaboration, without the false modesty that would have been its own kind of vanity.

Elder Thomas left.

Ruth remained in the room.

She looked at the floor.

The circle was still there. Faint, almost invisible, worn into the boards by feet that had moved in ways feet no longer moved here. She had never touched it. In all her years of witnessing, she had walked around it, had positioned her chair outside its edge, had observed it the way one observes a stain or a scar—something present, something past, something that required no action because it was already complete.

She crossed the room. She knelt at the edge of the worn circle.

Her hand moved before she decided to move it. Her fingertips touched the floor where the wear was deepest, where decades of turning feet had polished the grain smooth. The wood was cool. The smoothness was real. Under her fingers she could feel the difference between this wood and the wood around it—the circle marked not just by sight but by texture, by the thousand small abrasions of bodies moving in ways that had meaning.

She stayed there for a moment. Kneeling. Touching.

Then she pulled her hand back and stood.

She did not know what she had expected to feel. The wood was wood. The floor was floor. Whatever had worn it smooth was gone, had been gone for longer than Ruth had been alive, and no amount of touching would bring it back or explain what it had been or tell her why the memory of Clarissa had surfaced today after twenty years of silence.

She closed the window. She walked to the door.

She did not look back.

The afternoon passed. Ruth recorded the confessions in the ledger. Names and dates, nothing more. Sister Eunice, October 17, 1897. Sister Hannah, October 17, 1897. Sister Mercy. Sister Abigail. The names in their column, the dates in theirs, the record complete.

At supper, Ruth watched the household eat. Eunice was present, her manner calm, her appetite steady. She ate without the distracted picking that had characterized her meals in recent weeks. But Ruth, watching, could not tell what the steadiness meant. Relief, perhaps. Or something flatter—the composure of someone who had spoken what could be spoken and sealed away what could not. Hannah too seemed different, though Ruth could not say how. She sat beside Sister Mercy, nodding at the appropriate moments, her face attentive. Whether the attention was presence or performance, Ruth did not know.

After supper, Ruth made her evening rounds. The kitchen was clean, the fires banked, the doors secured. Each task completed, each role performed, each person in their place.

She returned to the office.

The ledger was open on the desk where she had left it. The day's confessions recorded, the names and dates in their proper columns, the evidence that the practice had been maintained. She should close it. She should extinguish the lamp and go to her room and sleep.

She sat down instead.

She looked at the page. The names. The dates. The record that held nothing of what had been spoken, nothing of what had almost been spoken, nothing of the pressure behind Eunice's eyes or the weight that had passed through Elder Patience's hands twenty years ago or the circle worn into the floor by feet that had once moved in ways that feet no longer moved.

Her pen was in her hand. She did not remember picking it up.

She turned to a fresh page. Not the page for tomorrow's assignments. Not the page for next week's schedule. A page at the back of the ledger, where nothing was recorded, where the paper was blank and waiting.

She wrote nothing.

She sat with the pen hovering over the empty page, the ink gathering at the nib, her hand not moving.

Clarissa had wept and said: "It needed to go somewhere."

Where did it go now? The resentment Eunice had spoken, the imaginings Hannah had confessed, the small failures of patience and attention that the others had offered—where did those go? They were spoken. They were received. They were released. But released into what? The room did not hold them. The elder did not rise and place his hands on shoulders and let the weight pass through. The words simply ended, and the silence returned, and the confessor departed lighter than they had arrived.

The friction was removed.

But the weight—

Ruth's hand moved. She made a single mark on the blank page. Not a word. Not a name or a date. Just a short horizontal line, like a dash, like a breath held and not released.

She looked at it.

The mark had no category. It could not be explained. If someone asked her what it meant, she would have no answer, because she did not know what it meant herself. She only knew that the page had been blank, and now it was not, and the difference between those two states was the only record she could make of what she had remembered and what she had touched and what she did not understand.

She closed the ledger.

The mark was inside it now. Hidden. Uncategorized. Present.

Ruth extinguished the lamp and sat in the darkness of the office, the closed ledger under her hands, the night settling over the buildings and the fields and the room where confession happened and the circle that remained worn into the floor.

The practice continued. The form remained.

And somewhere in the ledger, a single mark waited for a meaning.

Three weeks later, the mark was still there when the county men arrived.

CHAPTER FIVE

The Assessment

The wagon appeared on the road shortly after the morning meeting.

Ruth saw it from the office window, a dark shape moving through the November gray, the horse's breath visible in the cold air. Visitors were not common. Visitors with wagons were less common still. She watched as the vehicle approached, as it slowed at the gate, as two figures consulted something between them before continuing up the lane.

She met them at the door of the office building.

Two men. The elder was perhaps fifty, his coat well-made but worn at the cuffs, his hat the kind that county officials wore when they wished to appear respectable without appearing wealthy. The younger was perhaps twenty-five, carrying a leather case that bulged with papers. Neither smiled. Neither frowned. Their faces held the neutral composure of people performing a task they had performed many times before.

"Good morning," the elder said. "I am William Hartwell, assistant clerk for the county assessor's office. This is Mr. Davies, my secretary." He produced a letter from his coat pocket. "We are conducting a survey of communal and religious properties in the county. The state requires an updated record of such holdings. I believe notice was sent to your Elder Thomas some weeks ago."

Ruth took the letter. The paper was official, bearing the county seal and a date from late October. She had seen the correspondence. Elder Thomas had mentioned it briefly, without concern. A routine matter, he had said. Administrative.

"Yes," Ruth said. "We received notice. I am Sister Ruth Pelham. I keep the community's records. Elder Thomas asked that I assist you with your inquiry."

Hartwell nodded. "That will be satisfactory. We require only an accounting of membership, property, and general condition. The survey should not take more than an hour of your time."

"Please come in," Ruth said. "The meeting room will serve for our discussion."

She led them across the yard to the meeting house. The morning was cold, the sky a flat white that promised neither snow nor clearing. Their footsteps were loud on the frozen ground. Mr. Davies's pen case rattled slightly as he walked.

The meeting room was too large for three people.

Ruth had known this before, had felt it during morning meetings when eleven chairs occupied a space built for forty. But she felt it differently now, seeing the room through the eyes of strangers. The high ceiling. The walls that angled inward. The worn floor that showed patterns of movement that no longer occurred.

She gestured to the chairs she had arranged near the window, where the light was strongest. "Please, sit. I will answer what questions I can."

Hartwell sat. Davies sat beside him, opening his case and removing a sheaf of forms, a pen, a small bottle of ink. His movements were practiced, efficient. He did not look up as he prepared his materials.

"We will begin with membership," Hartwell said. He consulted his papers. "Our records indicate that the North Family of this community numbered eighteen members as of the last survey in 1889. Is that figure still accurate?"

"No," Ruth said. "The current membership is eleven."

Davies's pen moved. Hartwell made a small notation on his own paper.

"Eleven," Hartwell repeated. "And the composition? Male and female?"

"Six sisters. Five brothers."

"Ages?"

"The youngest is thirty-five. The eldest is eighty-one. The average age is fifty-nine years."

The pen moved. The numbers were recorded. Hartwell's expression did not change.

"And in the period since the last survey—eight years—how many new members have joined the community?"

Ruth considered the question. It was a simple question. It required a simple answer.

"None," she said.

"None," Hartwell repeated. He made another notation. "And departures? Deaths?"

"Seven deaths since 1889. No departures."

The arithmetic was clear. Eighteen minus seven equaled eleven. The figures aligned.

"I see," Hartwell said. "And are there any applications pending? Any inquiries from persons wishing to join?"

"No," Ruth said. "There are no applications pending."

Davies's pen scratched against the paper. The sound was steady, rhythmic, the sound of information being transferred from one form of record to another.

"We will move to property," Hartwell said. "The community holds three hundred and forty acres, according to the deed records. Is this still accurate?"

"Yes. The acreage has not changed since the original grant in 1842."

"And the current use of that land?"

Ruth recited the figures she knew by heart. "Forty acres under cultivation, reduced from sixty-five. Eighty-five acres fallow. Thirty acres of pasture. One hundred eighty-five acres of woodland, unchanged."

"Reduced from sixty-five," Hartwell said. "When was this reduction made?"

"Gradually, over the past ten years. As the membership declined, the cultivated area was adjusted to match available labor."

Hartwell nodded. The explanation was reasonable. The explanation required no further inquiry.

"Buildings," he said. "The property records indicate twelve structures. How many are currently in use?"

Ruth counted in her mind. "Six are in regular use. The main dwelling, the meeting house, the dairy, the laundry shed, the carpentry workshop, and the south barn for livestock. The remaining structures are used for storage or stand empty."

"Livestock?"

"Four cows. Twelve chickens. No horses. We hire transportation when needed."

"Primary sources of income?"

"Furniture sales. Herbal preparations. Some preserved goods sold to the surrounding towns."

"And these sources are sufficient?"

"They are adequate for our current needs," Ruth said. "We do not anticipate expansion."

Davies continued writing. His pen had not paused throughout the exchange.

"Leadership," Hartwell said. "The community is governed by—"

"Elder Thomas Whitfield. He has served as elder for thirty-one years."

"And in the event of Elder Whitfield's—" Hartwell paused. "In the event that Elder Whitfield is no longer able to serve, who would assume leadership?"

Ruth did not answer immediately.

The question was reasonable. Succession. Continuity. The mechanisms by which institutions persisted beyond individual lives. These were proper concerns for a county record.

She thought of the eleven names in the ledger. The ages. The capacities. The column that did not exist.

"The community would select a new elder according to our established practices," Ruth said finally. "The selection would be made by the remaining members in consultation with the Ministry at New Lebanon, if communication with them remains possible."

"If communication remains possible," Hartwell repeated. He made a note. "And among the current membership, is there a likely successor? Someone who has been prepared for leadership?"

"The selection would be made when the need arose," Ruth said. "I cannot speak to the outcome."

Hartwell accepted this. He moved on.

"Financial records," he said. "The county requires confirmation that the community maintains accurate accounts of income, expenditure, and property. Do such records exist?"

"Yes," Ruth said. "I maintain the community's ledger. All transactions are recorded. All property is inventoried annually."

"Would it be possible to examine this ledger?"

"Yes," she said. "I will bring it."

She rose and walked to the office building, leaving the two men in the meeting room. The cold air was sharp after the relative warmth of the enclosed space. She retrieved the ledger from its shelf, feeling the familiar weight of it, the soft leather binding worn smooth by decades of hands.

When she returned, Hartwell and Davies were speaking quietly. They stopped when she entered.

She placed the ledger on the table between them and opened it to the current year's entries. "The annual inventory is recorded here. Membership, property, stores, projections. The format has been consistent since the community's founding."

Hartwell leaned forward and examined the pages. His eyes moved down the columns, pausing at the membership list, at the property inventory, at the summary that Ruth had written only weeks before. Gradual reduction in capacity. No new admissions anticipated.

"This is thorough," he said.

"The record must be accurate," Ruth said.

Hartwell nodded. He turned back several pages, examining earlier entries, earlier years. The membership figures from 1890. From 1885. From 1880. The slow contraction visible in the columns, the numbers declining year by year, name by name.

"You have maintained this yourself?" he asked.

"For twenty-three years. Before me, Sister Eliza kept the record. Before her, others."

"The handwriting changes," Hartwell observed. "But the format remains the same."

"Yes," Ruth said. "The format remains the same."

Davies had stopped writing. He was looking at the ledger. Ruth could not read his expression. She did not try.

Hartwell closed the ledger and pushed it gently back toward Ruth. "The record is well-kept."

"Thank you," Ruth said.

"Would it be possible to see the property itself? A brief tour of the buildings and grounds? For the purposes of the survey, we must confirm that the structures are maintained, that the land is being used as described."

"Of course," Ruth said. "I will show you what you wish to see."

She led them out of the meeting house and across the yard. The tour was brief, as Hartwell had promised. The main dwelling, where Ruth pointed out the kitchen and the common areas, without entering. The workshop, where Brother Daniel's bench stood empty but maintained, his tools arranged on their pegs, his unfinished work covered with cloth. The dairy, where the equipment was clean and orderly, the butter churn standing ready.

They walked past the dormitory building, the one that had once housed the younger members, the novices, the new arrivals who no longer arrived. The windows were dark. The door was closed.

"This building," Hartwell said. "It is not in use?"

"It has not been occupied for seven years," Ruth said. "We maintain it. The roof is sound."

Hartwell nodded. Davies made a note.

They continued past the herb house, past the seed house, past the visitors' quarters that had not held visitors in longer than Ruth could easily remember. Each building was noted. Each condition was recorded.

The tour ended at the gate, where the wagon waited, the horse standing patient in the cold.

"I believe we have what we need," Hartwell said. He extended his hand, and Ruth shook it. His grip was firm, professional, the handshake of someone completing a transaction. "Thank you for your assistance, Sister Ruth."

"I am glad the survey was satisfactory," Ruth said.

"The community will be noted in our records as declining but orderly," Hartwell said. "There are no irregularities that would require further inquiry."

"That should be sufficient for our purposes," he said.

Davies closed his case. The papers were secured, the ink bottle stoppered, the pen wiped clean, and returned to its holder.

"Good day, Sister Ruth," Hartwell said.

"Good day," Ruth said.

She watched as they climbed into the wagon, as Hartwell took the reins, as the horse began to move. The wagon rolled down the lane, past the gate, onto the road that led back to the town.

The road was empty.

Ruth returned to the office.

The afternoon continued. The midday meal was served in the usual silence. The household did not ask about the visitors. Ruth did not speak of them.

She sat at her desk and opened the ledger to the page where she recorded events of note.

She wrote: November 14, 1897. County assessment conducted. Records reviewed. Property surveyed. No irregularities noted. No action required.

Ruth let the ink dry. She closed the ledger and returned it to its shelf.

The afternoon light was fading. Somewhere in the kitchen, the evening meal was being prepared. Somewhere in the workshop, tools hung waiting on their pegs.

Ruth turned from the shelf and began her afternoon rounds.

Declining but orderly.

The assessment was complete.

CHAPTER SIX

The Long View

The first frost came in the third week of November, earlier than expected. Ruth woke to find the windows edged with ice, the patterns delicate and precise, the kind of frost that would melt by midmorning but that signaled the turn toward true winter. She lay in bed for a moment before the bell, looking at the frost, at the way the early light caught in the crystals and made them glow. Then the bell rang, and she rose, and the day began.

The cold had settled into the buildings overnight. The hallway floors were frigid beneath her shoes, the air sharp in a way that made breathing feel like work. She could see her breath in the dim light as she walked toward the stairs, small clouds that formed and dissolved, formed and dissolved.

Sister Catherine's cough was worse. Ruth could hear it before she reached the stairs. A deep, rattling sound that carried through the closed door, through the hallway, through the particular silence of early morning. The physician had come twice now. Rest was prescribed, and warmth, and the tinctures that Sister Eunice prepared from the herbs she had dried in the autumn. The cough did not improve. It did not worsen, either, not in any way that could be measured or addressed. It simply continued, present now in every morning's sounds, part of the household's rhythm in a way it had not been a month ago.

Ruth paused at Catherine's door but did not knock. There was nothing to offer that had not already been offered. The fire in Catherine's room would need building up. She made a note of this and added it to the morning's tasks.

The kitchen was already active when Ruth arrived. Sister Mercy stood at the great stove, her movements slower than they had been even a month ago, the careful deliberation of someone conserving strength for the tasks that required it most. Her hands, Ruth noticed, trembled slightly when she lifted the heavy kettle. Not much. Not enough to spill. But the tremor was there, visible in the steam that rose from the water.

"The oats are nearly ready," Mercy said without turning. "Hannah has the bread sliced. We'll need more wood for the fire before midday. The cold is deeper than I expected."

Ruth nodded and made the note. Wood for the kitchen, for Catherine's room, for the meeting hall.

"I'll see to it," Ruth said.

She found Brother Joseph in the woodshed, already loading the small cart that was used to move fuel from building to building. He was sixty-three, still strong in the way that men who had worked with their bodies all their lives remained strong, but slower now than he had been. The loading took longer. He lifted each piece of wood with deliberation, settling it into the cart with care, pausing between pieces to let his breath return to its normal rhythm. Ruth remembered when he had made the rounds twice each morning during cold spells, the cart moving briskly across the frozen yard, the work completed before the breakfast bell. Now he would make one round, and it would take most of the morning.

"The main dwelling first," Ruth said. "Sister Catherine's room needs particular attention. Then the kitchen, then the meeting hall."

Brother Joseph nodded. He did not speak. He rarely spoke, had grown quieter over the years as his hearing had diminished. He loaded the cart with the steady rhythm of long practice, each piece of wood placed precisely, the load balanced for the walk across the yard. When the cart was full, he gripped the handles and lifted, and Ruth saw the effort in his shoulders, the slight tremor in his arms that echoed the tremor she had seen in Mercy's hands. The cart moved forward, the wheels creaking against the cold, Brother Joseph's breath clouding in the morning air as he walked.

Ruth watched him cross the yard, the pace measured, unhurried, the pace of someone who knew how much strength he had and how far that strength needed to carry him. Then she returned to the main building.

At breakfast, she counted the household as she always counted. Ten present. Sister Catherine absent, resting. The number had been ten for six months now, since Brother Peter had passed in the spring. Before that, it had been eleven. The tables held place settings for more, had always held place settings for more, the extra places maintained because the tables had been built for a larger household, and there was no reason to rebuild them for a smaller one.

Elder Thomas spoke at the morning meeting about the winter preparations, about the adequacy of the stores, and about the schedule of tasks that would carry the community through the cold months. His voice was steady, his words measured, his manner unchanged from how it had been when Ruth had first heard him speak forty years ago. But his movements were slower now. The walk to the front of the meeting room took more steps than it once had, each step deliberate, considered.

"Brother Daniel has returned to full duties in the woodshop," Elder Thomas said. "The orders for spring will need attention through the winter months. Brother William will continue to assist." He paused, the pause longer than it would have been a year ago. "Sister Catherine remains in the infirmary. Her duties in the sewing room will be covered by Sister Hannah until her recovery is complete."

Ruth heard this and noted it. Hannah in the sewing room. The role would be filled. The work would continue.

After the meeting, Ruth returned to the office and opened the ledger where the assignments were recorded. She turned back through the pages, not looking for anything specific, simply observing. The names appeared in columns, each name attached to tasks, each task attached to dates. The handwriting changed as she moved backward through time. Her own hand giving way to Sister Patience's, Sister Patience's to Sister Clarissa's, the record extending back through decades of careful notation.

The format had been established by Mother Lucy in 1821. Ruth knew this because she had seen the earlier records, the ones kept before the format was standardized. They were in the archive room on the third floor, stored in boxes that were rarely opened. She had looked at them once, years ago, when she was new to this work and curious about what had come before.

The old records were different. Names and dates, yes, but also other things. What gifts each person carried. What they brought to meeting. What moved through them when the spirit moved. Sister Abigail Whitmore, the records said, received the gift of placement. She knew where things should go. Brother Isaiah received songs that had never been sung before. Sister Martha spoke in the language of angels for three hours on a winter morning in 1799.

The old format recorded what the spirit did. The new format recorded what people did.

She turned more pages. Names with dates beside them. Some dates marked arrivals. More marked departures. The columns for arrivals had empty space beneath the last entries. The columns for departures continued to the present page.

Ruth closed the ledger and began her morning rounds.

The sewing room was quiet when she entered. Hannah sat at the window where Catherine usually sat, the light falling on her work, her needle moving through fabric with careful attention. The stitches were even competent, adequate. They would hold a winter's wearing. They were not Catherine's stitches. Not the nearly invisible mending that had made the community's work sought after, not the fine embroidery that decorated the sale goods. But they would serve.

"The mending is progressing," Hannah said, not looking up. Her voice was tight with concentration, the effort of the work visible in the set of her shoulders, in the careful way she guided the needle. "Brother Joseph's coat is finished. I've started on the winter linens."

Ruth examined the finished coat. The seams were secure, the patches invisible from the outside, the work serviceable.

"The silk thread," Ruth said. "Has it been stored properly?"

Hannah's hands paused. "In the upper cabinet. With the other supplies for the fine work."

Ruth nodded. The fine work. The work that Catherine could still envision but could no longer execute. The supplies waited in their cabinet.

"Continue with the mending," Ruth said. "The winter linens are the priority."

She left the sewing room and walked down the hallway toward the workshop. Through the windows, she could see the yard, the frost still white on the grass in the shadows where the sun had not yet reached, the paths between buildings marked by darker lines where feet had walked and compressed the frost into something closer to ice.

She passed the door to the children's dwelling and stopped.

She had not intended to stop. Her rounds did not include this building. There was no reason to enter, no task that required attention, no person whose work needed checking. The building had been closed for eleven years, since the last of the children who had been raised here had grown and either committed to the community or returned to the world. The door was closed as it had been closed for eleven years.

Ruth stood at the door. Her hand rested on the latch.

She lifted the latch and pushed the door open.

The air inside was colder than the air outside, the kind of cold that accumulated in closed spaces, undisturbed by fire or breath or the warmth of bodies moving through. The windows were intact, the glass clean, the light falling through in pale rectangles that illuminated the room beyond.

The room had been a dormitory. Small beds lined the walls, eight on each side, the frames built low to the ground so that small bodies could climb in and out without assistance. The beds were stripped to their ticking now, the linens folded and stored elsewhere, the mattresses bare. The frames remained because there was no reason to remove them. They were well-made, built to last, built by hands that had expected children to sleep in them for generations.

Ruth stepped inside. Her footsteps echoed in the empty space. She walked down the center aisle between the beds, her eyes moving over the room.

She looked at the floor.

The floor was worn differently here. Not the smooth paths of adult feet walking in measured steps, not the arcs and curves of the meeting room, not the straight lines of hallways traveled in formation. The wear here was chaotic. Patterns that seemed random, that crossed and recrossed, that spiraled and stopped and started again. The wood was lighter in patches, darker in others, the record of movement that had not followed any pattern the adult mind would recognize.

Children had run here.

Ruth stood in the center of the room and looked at the floor. Children had run. Before they learned to walk with intention, before their bodies were shaped to the discipline the community required, before the formation began. They had run because running was what children did, because the body arrived in the world wanting to move, wanting to play, wanting the pure physical joy of motion without purpose.

The running had worn the floor in patterns that looked chaotic now. But they had not been chaotic then. They had been play. They had been the body before the body learned what it was for.

Ruth turned and walked back to the door, her footsteps loud in the silence, and she closed the door behind her and stood for a moment in the cold November air.

Eleven years. The building had been closed for eleven years. No new children had come, because no new members had come, and the children who might have been born here could not be born here because the life they had chosen did not permit the making of children.

The building would stand. The beds would remain. The floor would hold its record of running feet until the floor itself was gone.

Ruth continued her rounds.

The workshop was warm. Brother Daniel kept the fire high when he was working, the heat necessary for the glue to set properly. He was at his bench when Ruth entered, his hands moving over a piece of cherry wood with the sureness of long practice. Seventy-one years old, and his hands still knew what they knew.

Brother William worked at the smaller bench near the window. His movements were different. Careful where Daniel's were confident, considered where Daniel's were instinctive. The chair he was building had clean lines, solid joinery, adequate craftsmanship. It would hold. It would serve.

"The orders for spring," Ruth said. "Are they proceeding on schedule?"

Brother Daniel looked up. His face was thinner than it had been before the illness, the bones more visible beneath the skin, but his eyes were clear. "The writing desk is nearly complete. The chairs will take longer. William is learning."

William did not look up from his work. His hands continued their careful movement, the plane sliding across wood, the shavings curling and falling. Learning. At forty-seven, he was learning what Daniel had learned at twenty, what Daniel had perfected over fifty years of daily practice.

Ruth watched them work for a moment longer, then left the workshop.

She stopped at Catherine's room in the late morning. The door was open now. The fire had been built up, the room warm enough that fresh air was welcome. Catherine sat in the chair by the window, a blanket over her lap, her hands folded and still. Her hands were never still anymore when there was work to do. The stillness meant the day stretched before her with nothing to fill it.

"The frost was heavy this morning," Catherine said. Her voice was thinner than it had been, worn by the coughing, by the weeks of illness. "I could see it on the window. The patterns were beautiful."

Ruth sat in the chair across from her.

"Hannah is managing the sewing room," Ruth said. "The winter mending is progressing."

Catherine nodded. The nod was slow, as if even that small motion required thought. "Hannah is capable. She will learn what she can learn." She coughed, the sound wet and deep. When the coughing passed, she did not continue the thought. She looked out the window at the frost that was finally beginning to melt in the late morning sun.

Ruth waited. The silence held. Catherine's breathing was audible in the quiet room, the slight rasp that had not been there a month ago.

"The light is good today," Catherine said finally. "Even with the cold."

"Yes," Ruth said. "It is."

She sat with Catherine for a few minutes more, neither of them speaking. The fire crackled. The frost continued its slow retreat from the window glass. Outside, Brother

Joseph's cart was visible crossing the yard again, emptier now, moving toward the woodshed for another load.

Ruth rose. "I will check on you this afternoon."

Catherine nodded, her eyes still on the window. "The physician comes tomorrow."

Ruth left the room and closed the door behind her.

The afternoon brought the work that afternoons always brought. Ruth updated the supply lists, noting what would be needed from the trustees' next visit. Flour, sugar, salt, thread, candles, and medicine for Catherine. She wrote the requests in her careful hand, the letters small and even, the list precise.

She opened the ledger that tracked the household's capacity. This was a different ledger from the assignment book, a record she had begun keeping three years ago when the pattern had become clear enough to require documentation. The ledger had columns for each member of the community, rows for each category of function. Active. Limited. Reduced. Inactive.

She reviewed the entries. The column for Active had grown shorter over the years. The column for Limited had grown longer. The column for Inactive held only two names now. Sister Catherine. Brother Thomas, whose role was spiritual rather than physical.

There was no column for Restored to Previous Duty.

At the bottom of the page, she had written a summary: Gradual reduction in capacity. External assistance anticipated. No new admissions.

Ruth closed the ledger and continued with the afternoon's work.

She wrote the assignment schedule for the coming week. The names filled the columns. Each person matched to each task, the work distributed among the available hands. The same names appeared in multiple columns. Eunice in the herb garden and the preserving shed. Hannah in the kitchen and the sewing room. Mercy in the kitchen and the supervision of stores. The columns balanced. They were always balanced because Ruth made them balance.

At supper, Ruth watched the household eat. Nine at the table. Sister Catherine was taking her meal in her room. The food was simple and adequate, prepared with care by hands that moved more slowly than they once had, served in the silence that was customary, consumed in the rhythm of a community that had eaten together in this room for a hundred years.

After supper, Ruth made her evening rounds. The kitchen was clean, the fires banked in the main rooms, built up in Catherine's room, where the warmth needed to last through the night. The doors were secured. The animals were fed and sheltered.

She stopped at the assignment board in the hallway and studied the names she had written there that morning. Tomorrow's work, arranged and assigned. She erased the board and wrote the next day's assignments, the chalk moving across the slate in the familiar rhythm.

She paused at the window at the end of the hallway. Through the glass, she could see the children's dwelling, dark now, its windows catching no light because there was no light inside to catch. The building stood where it had stood for eighty years, solid, maintained, empty.

Ruth turned from the window and walked to her room.

The hallway was quiet, the household settling into sleep. Behind one door, Catherine coughed. The sound muffled now, part of the night's texture. Behind the closed doors of the empty rooms, nothing.

Ruth prepared for bed. The sequence was familiar, automatic, unchanged. She knelt in prayer, the words the same words she had spoken every night for forty-three years. She asked for guidance in her duties, for strength for the work, for patience with the order that held them all.

She rose and climbed into bed. The sheets were cool, then warm. The room was dark. Across the room, Sister Abigail slept, her breathing steady, her rest untroubled.

Ruth lay in the darkness and listened. The house settling. The wind outside. The particular quiet of a place at rest.

Tomorrow, she would update the entries. Tomorrow, she would balance the assignments against the hands available. Tomorrow, the work would continue because the work was what they did, and doing it was prayer, and prayer did not require an audience or a future or anything beyond the doing itself.

The children's dwelling stood in the darkness. Its door closed. Its beds empty. Its floor holding what floors hold.

The faithfulness was in the continuing, not in the counting. God knew the numbers. God held the future. Her work was the present, and the present was full, and she would meet it when the bell rang.

She closed her eyes.

The frost would be heavy again by morning.

CHAPTER SEVEN

Adjustment

The morning began as mornings always began: with the bell, with the dark, with the sequence of waking and dressing that had become so familiar over forty-three years that Ruth could perform it without thought, her hands finding the cloth and pins and ties in the darkness as surely as they would find them in full light. Across the room, Sister Abigail stirred and began her own preparations. Neither spoke. Speech would come later, when there was reason for it.

The hallway was cold, the November air pressing against the windows with the particular insistence of a winter that had arrived early and intended to stay. Ruth walked the familiar path to the stairs, her shoes making their usual soft sounds on the pine boards, her hand finding the rail at the same worn spot where thousands of hands had found it before. The routine held. The routine always held.

In the kitchen, the fires had been started. Sister Mercy was at the stove, her back to the door, her hands engaged in the work they had been engaged in for thirty-one years. The kettle was heating. The oats were measured and waiting. The morning was proceeding as it should.

Ruth stood in the doorway and watched, as she often watched when she arrived before the others. Watching was part of her work. Observation preceded arrangement, and arrangement required that she know what was there to be arranged.

The kettle slipped.

Not far. Not dangerously. Sister Mercy's hands caught it before anything spilled, before the weight of the boiling water could shift past the point of recovery. But Ruth saw it from the doorway. The tremor, the adjustment, the small negotiation between intention and execution that had not been necessary a year ago, or six months ago, or perhaps even last month. The kettle found its place on the stove, the water began its work, and Mercy's hands moved on to the next task as if nothing had happened.

Ruth did not mention it. She continued her morning round, checking the bread that was rising, noting the supplies that would need replenishment, observing the rhythm of work that proceeded as it always proceeded. Sister Hannah was at the vegetable station, her knife moving through carrots with the steady pace of someone who had learned a task but not yet made it automatic. The pace was adequate. The cuts were even. The work was being done.

She left the kitchen and continued through the house.

The morning was cold, the November air sharp against the windows, the frost that had become familiar over the past weeks still visible in the shadows where the sun had not yet reached. She followed the day's circuit as she always did. The sewing room where Hannah's mending waited for the afternoon hours. The office where the ledgers held their patient record of everything that had been done and everything that remained to be done. The house was functioning. The people were functioning. The work continued.

But the image of the kettle stayed with her. The tremor. The recovery. The small moment that had been visible only because she had been watching, only because watching was what she did.

She returned to the office and opened the assignment ledger. The entries for the kitchen stretched back through years of careful notation. Who had worked which hours, who had prepared which meals, who had carried which responsibilities. Mercy's name appeared in nearly every entry for the past thirty-one years, the handwriting changing as different keepers had maintained the record, but the name constant. Sister Mercy, kitchen. Sister Mercy, morning meal. Sister Mercy, stores. The work had been hers for so long that the work and the person had become difficult to separate.

Ruth turned to a fresh page and began the calculations she had been avoiding.

The kitchen required certain tasks. The tasks required certain capacities. The capacities required certain bodies. This was not philosophy; it was arithmetic. The lifting of pots, the carrying of water, the stirring that went on for hours as soups and stews developed their flavors. Each task made demands, and the demands did not diminish simply because the body that met them had begun to change.

She listed the tasks in one column, the time each required in another. She noted which tasks could be performed seated and which required standing, which demanded strength, and which demanded only patience. She noted which tasks Mercy had always done herself and which she had delegated to Hannah, and she observed that the delegation had increased over the past months, the heavier work shifting quietly from one set of hands to another without anyone naming what was happening.

The columns filled. The picture clarified.

She turned back through the ledger, looking at the entries from a year ago, from two years ago, from five. The assignments had been the same. Mercy in the kitchen, morning and afternoon. Mercy responsible for the stores, the preparation, the maintenance of standards that the community had upheld for a century. The entries showed no change because there had been no change to show. The work had been constant. Only the body doing it had altered.

The kettle had not slipped because Mercy was careless. The kettle had slipped because the hands that held it were not the hands that had held it a year ago, and the year before that, and the twenty-nine years before that. The hands were the same hands, attached to the same person, guided by the same mind that had always guided them.

Ruth closed the ledger. Through the window, she could see the yard, the woodshed, the path to the kitchen building where smoke rose from the chimney in the thin, steady line that meant the fires were burning well.

She would need to speak with Elder Thomas.

The conversation happened that afternoon, in the small room off the meeting hall where such conversations always happened. Elder Thomas sat in his usual chair, his posture still straight despite the years, his attention complete. Ruth sat across from him and spoke plainly, as plainness was what the situation required.

"Sister Mercy's hands are not what they were," she said. "I have observed this for some months now. The tremor is more pronounced. The heavy work takes longer. This morning, the kettle." She paused, finding the precise words. "The kettle required her to catch it. She did. But the catching was necessary in a way it would not have been before."

Elder Thomas listened without interrupting. This was his way. To receive information fully before responding, to let the speaker complete what they had come to say.

"The kitchen work continues," Ruth said. "Sister Hannah is learning. She is capable, and her capability grows. But the weight of the work falls where it has always fallen, and the body that carries it is no longer." She stopped again. The words she needed were simple, but speaking them felt like crossing a threshold. "The body is no longer sufficient to the weight."

The silence held. Elder Thomas's face showed nothing but attention, the patient regard that had characterized his leadership for as long as Ruth had known him. When he spoke, his voice was measured.

"What adjustment do you propose?"

Ruth had prepared for this question. The answer had been forming in her mind since the morning, since the kettle, since the tremor that had been visible only because she had been watching.

"Sister Mercy should be relieved of the heavy labor," she said. "The lifting, the carrying, the work that requires sustained strength. Her judgment remains. Her knowledge remains. She can guide, advise, oversee. But the physical work should pass to Sister Hannah, who is capable of bearing it."

"Sister Hannah has been in the kitchen for—"

"Twelve years. She came to us at twenty-three. She has learned what Mercy has taught her, and she continues to learn. Her hands are steady. Her back is strong. Her instincts are not

Mercy's instincts. They may never be. But she can lift a kettle without the lifting requiring negotiation."

Elder Thomas was silent for a moment. His hands rested on the arms of his chair, the fingers still, the posture of someone considering rather than preparing to speak. Ruth waited. The waiting was part of the process. Decisions made too quickly were decisions made without the full weight of thought.

"And Sister Mercy's understanding of this change?" he asked finally.

"I have not spoken to her. I would not propose without your counsel."

Elder Thomas nodded slowly, the nod of someone considering rather than agreeing. "Sister Mercy has served the kitchen for thirty-one years. The work has been hers. The meals we have eaten, the stores we have kept, the standards we have maintained. These are her work, made material through her hands."

"Yes," Ruth said.

"And now her hands are changing."

"Yes."

The silence returned. Through the window, the afternoon light was beginning to lengthen, the shadows stretching across the yard as the sun descended toward the western hills. Somewhere in the kitchen, Mercy was working, her hands moving through the tasks they had performed thousands of times, her body negotiating with itself about what it could still do and what it could no longer do without cost.

"The adjustment is appropriate," Elder Thomas said finally. "The body has its seasons. Mother Ann taught this, and we have held it to be true. To ask of the body what it can no longer give is not faith; it is denial. Sister Mercy has given decades of faithful service. What remains is to ensure that her remaining years are spent in work that suits her present capacity, not in struggle against what cannot be changed."

The body has its seasons. Ruth heard the phrase and felt it settle into place, as it always settled, as it had settled for a hundred years whenever bodies changed, and work was redistributed. The phrase was Mother Ann's. It had been spoken at every transition Ruth had witnessed, every adjustment, every moment when someone moved from one capacity to another.

"I will speak with her," she said.

"Speak with her as you would wish to be spoken with," Elder Thomas said. "Not as loss, but as acknowledgment. Not as ending, but as change. The work continues. Her place in the work continues. Only the nature of her contribution changes, and it changes because change is what bodies do. The body has its seasons, and this is hers."

Ruth nodded and rose. The conversation was complete. What remained was the harder work. The speaking, the receiving, the moment when the adjustment became real in the only way that mattered: between persons, face to face, word by word.

She found Mercy in the kitchen, as she knew she would. The afternoon meal was finished, the cleaning underway, the steady rhythm of work that characterized every hour of every day in this place. Hannah was at the sink, her arms deep in the wash water, her movements methodical. Mercy stood at the work table, her hands sorting dried beans into the categories that would determine how they were used. The whole ones for soups, the broken ones for grinding, the discolored ones for the compost that fed the garden.

The sorting was work Mercy had done for years. It required attention but not strength. Her hands moved through the beans with the efficiency of long practice, the tremor visible only when Ruth looked for it, present only in the moments between motions when the hands were still.

"Sister Mercy," Ruth said. "When you have finished, I would like to speak with you."

Mercy looked up. Her face was calm, her expression the neutral regard that years in the community had cultivated. "I am nearly done. The beans can wait."

She wiped her hands on her apron and followed Ruth out of the kitchen, through the cold yard, to the small room where

Ruth conducted the conversations that her role required. The room was plain. Two chairs, a small table, a window that looked out on the same yard they had just crossed. Ruth gestured to one chair and took the other.

"I have spoken with Elder Thomas," Ruth said. "About the kitchen work. About the arrangements that serve our needs best."

Mercy's face did not change. She sat with her hands folded in her lap, her posture straight, her attention complete. Whatever she felt, anticipation, concern, resignation, did not show in her expression.

"I have observed," Ruth continued, "that the heavy work takes more from you than it once did. The lifting. The carrying. The sustained effort that the kitchen requires." She paused, finding the words that were true without being cruel. "Your hands are not what they were. This is not failure. The body has its seasons. Mother Ann taught us this. It is the natural change, the seasons that all flesh moves through."

Mercy nodded once, the nod neither agreement nor disagreement, simply acknowledgment that the words had been heard.

"The proposal is this," Ruth said. "The heavy labor passes to Sister Hannah. She is capable, and her capability grows. You remain in the kitchen. Your judgment, your knowledge, your years of understanding what the work requires. But the lifting, the carrying, the tasks that strain. These become hers. You guide. You oversee. You ensure that the standards you have maintained continue to be maintained. But you no longer bear the weight yourself."

The silence stretched. Ruth watched Mercy's face, looking for the signs of resistance, of grief, of the protest that would mean the adjustment had been proposed too quickly or too harshly. But Mercy's expression remained composed, her hands still folded, her breathing even.

"I have felt it," Mercy said finally. Her voice was quiet but clear, the voice of someone who had thought about what she was saying before she said it. "The kettle this morning. You saw. I saw that you saw. My hands do not obey as they once did. The work I could do without thought now requires thought, and sometimes the thought is not fast enough."

Ruth waited. There was more coming, she could feel it, and the speaking of it was Mercy's right.

"Thirty-one years," Mercy said. "I have been in that kitchen thirty-one years. I came when I was young, when my hands were quick, and my back was strong. I learned from Sister Patience, who learned from Sister Clarissa, who learned from whoever came before. The knowledge passed to me, and I thought." She stopped, her lips pressing together briefly before she continued. "I thought I would pass it on the same way. That I would grow old in that kitchen and teach what I knew to whoever came next, and they would carry it forward after I was gone."

"You will teach," Ruth said. "That is precisely what you will do. Hannah needs what you know. The meals we have eaten for thirty-one years. She cannot make them without your guidance. The work changes, but the teaching continues."

Mercy's hands moved in her lap, the fingers interlacing briefly before returning to their folded position. "The body has its seasons," she said quietly. "I have heard this phrase my whole life here. I have said it to others when their seasons changed. I did not know how it would feel to have it said to me."

Ruth did not respond immediately. The words were accurate. The phrase had been said, and the phrase was true, and the truth of it did not change how it felt to receive it.

"It is kind," Mercy continued. "The way you have spoken. The way Elder Thomas has decided. It is kind to frame it as a continuation rather than ending."

Ruth heard this without responding. Kindness was part of how the adjustment had been conceived, how the conversation had been constructed. But kindness was not the whole of it. The adjustment was also practical, necessary, the response that a well-ordered community made when circumstances required response. That the response was kind did not make it less inevitable. That the words were gentle did not change what the words described.

"The schedule will change beginning tomorrow," Ruth said. "You will come to the kitchen at the same hour. The work will proceed as it has always proceeded. But when the heavy tasks arise. The lifting of pots, the carrying of supplies, the work that demands what your hands no longer give freely. You will direct, and Hannah will perform."

Mercy nodded again. The nod was slower this time, weighted with something Ruth could not quite name. "I understand."

"Is there more you wish to say?"

The question was genuine. Ruth had learned, over years of such conversations, that the speaking was sometimes more important than the hearing, that what people needed most was the space to voice what they carried, whether or not the voicing changed anything.

Mercy was quiet for a long moment. Her hands lay still in her lap, the hands that had lifted and carried and stirred for thirty-one years, the hands that would now direct rather than perform. Ruth watched them and saw what Mercy must have seen every day for the past months. The slight tremor, the skin grown looser over the bones, the small betrayals of a body that had served faithfully and was now serving differently.

"I thought I had more time," Mercy said finally. Her voice was steady, but there was something beneath the steadiness, something that moved like water beneath ice. "I knew the change was coming. Everyone knows. But I thought. I thought there would be more warning. More gradual. A slow loosening, not a morning when the kettle simply." She stopped, her lips pressing together briefly. "I did not expect it to happen so clearly. So suddenly visible."

"It was visible only because I was watching," Ruth said. "To anyone else, to Hannah, to the others. The kettle was lifted, the water was poured, and the morning proceeded. No one else saw."

"But you saw." Mercy's eyes met Ruth's, and in them Ruth saw the thing she had not wanted to see: the recognition that what had been private was now shared, that the adjustment that felt like ending was now official, recorded, real.

"Yes," Ruth said. "I saw."

The silence held. Through the window, the afternoon light continued its slow descent, the shadows lengthening across the yard, the day proceeding toward evening as days always proceeded, regardless of what conversations happened within them.

"No," Mercy said at last. "You have spoken what needed to be spoken. I will do what needs to be done." She rose from her chair, her movements careful in the way that movements became careful when the body could no longer be trusted to perform without supervision. "The beans are waiting. Hannah will need guidance on the evening meal."

She paused at the door, her hand on the frame, her back to Ruth. She did not turn around. "Thank you," she said. "For speaking as you did. For framing it as continuation rather than ending. Even if." She stopped. Whatever she had been about to say, she chose not to say it. "Thank you."

She left the room without looking back. Ruth sat for a moment in the empty space, listening to the footsteps recede across the yard, the sound of the kitchen door opening and closing, the return to work that characterized every transition here. The conversation was complete. The adjustment was made.

She rose and returned to the office.

The ledger was open on the desk where she had left it that morning. Ruth sat down and turned to the page where the assignments were recorded. She found Mercy's name, the familiar entry that had appeared in some form for thirty-one years, and she drew a thin line beneath it.

She did not cross out the name. That would come later, when Mercy no longer worked in the kitchen at all, when the change that had begun today reached its natural conclusion. For now, the name remained, the role remained, only the nature of the role had changed.

She dipped her pen in the ink and moved to write the new notation beside Mercy's name.

Her hand paused.

The pen hovered over the page, the ink gathering at the nib, the moment stretching. Ruth looked at Mercy's name, at the thirty-one years of entries that preceded this one, at the space where the new words would go. Supervision. Guidance. Oversight.

The words were accurate. They described what Mercy would do, what her days would contain, how her presence in the kitchen would continue even as the substance of that presence transformed.

But the words were also final.

Her hand did not move. The pen waited. The ink gathered.

She thought of Mercy's hands sorting beans. She thought of the kettle slipping and recovering. She thought of the phrase that had governed every such transition for a hundred years: the body has its seasons. The phrase was true. The phrase was comfort. The phrase was what the system said to make the change bearable, to make the loss feel like progression, to make the ending feel like continuation.

Her hand moved. The pen touched the page. She wrote: supervision, guidance, oversight.

She looked at what she had written. The ink was drying. The words were fixed.

The hesitation was not recorded. Only the adjustment remained.

Ruth closed the ledger.

She turned to the column where reassignments were tracked. The column had no heading for "temporary." There was no space for noting that an adjustment might be reversed, that a change might be changed back.

Ruth looked at the column for a long moment. She had maintained this ledger for seventeen years, had written thousands of entries, had recorded births and deaths and arrivals and departures and every small shift in the arrangement of labor that kept the community functioning. In all that time, she had never written a notation that said "restored to previous duty." Never recorded a return to what had been. The column moved in one direction because bodies moved in one direction, and the work passed from hand to hand because that was the nature of hands, and the nature of work, and the nature of time.

The ledger assumed what the community assumed: that capacity diminished rather than restored, that the work passed forward because it could not pass backward. There was no form for recovery. There was no process for reversal. There was only the next entry, and the next, and the next, each one building on what came before.

Ruth noted the date beside the new assignment. November 22, 1897. The date when Mercy's role had changed. The date when the kitchen passed, in practice if not in name, from one generation to the next.

She closed the ledger and sat in the quiet office.

The light through the window was golden now, the late afternoon sun casting long shadows across the desk, across the ledger, across her hands where they rested on the leather binding. Her hands were still capable. They held pens, they turned pages, they performed the work that her role required. But she was sixty-two years old, and the work she did was not the work of lifting and carrying. The work she did was the work of recording, of arranging, of ensuring that the system continued to function as the people within it aged and changed and eventually stopped.

She thought about Mercy in the kitchen, sorting beans while Hannah washed dishes. The beans would be sorted properly. Mercy's judgment had not diminished, only her hands. The dishes would be washed thoroughly. Hannah was learning, and her learning was adequate. The kitchen would function tomorrow as it had functioned today, and the next day as it had functioned the day before. The meals would be prepared, the household fed, the work continued.

Nothing was lost. Something was finalized.

Ruth rose from the desk and walked to the window. The yard was empty in the late light, the buildings casting their long shadows across the grass, the smoke from the kitchen chimney still rising in its thin, steady line. Somewhere in one of those buildings, Mercy was teaching Hannah what she knew. Somewhere, the knowledge was passing from one set of hands to another, the transfer that had happened countless times before in this place, that would happen as long as the place continued.

This was how it worked. This was how it had always worked.

The body has its seasons. The system continued.

The evening meal was the same as every evening meal. The household gathered, the food was served, the silence held except for the necessary words. Ruth watched, as she always watched, and saw what she expected to see.

Mercy sat in her usual place. Her plate held the usual portions. Her hands managed the spoon and the bread with the usual competence that eating required. She did not look different. She did not appear diminished or reduced. She ate as she had always eaten, and when the meal was finished, she rose and returned to the kitchen to oversee the cleaning, to guide Hannah through the tasks that closed out the day.

But something had changed. Ruth could see it in the way Mercy moved. Not faster or slower, not more carefully or less, but differently. The way a person moves when they know they are being watched. The way a person moves when they are performing a role rather than inhabiting it. Mercy was still Mercy. The kitchen was still the kitchen. But the relationship between them had shifted, and the shift was visible to anyone who knew how to look.

Hannah moved with more certainty now. Ruth noticed this too. The announcement had not been made, would not be made. Such things were not announced but simply became true through practice. But Hannah had understood. Her hands lifted the heavier dishes without hesitation. Her arms carried the stacked plates to the kitchen without looking for assistance. The transfer had begun, and the beginning was already becoming normal.

Ruth watched her go and felt nothing she could name. The adjustment had been made. The work had been redistributed. The schedule would reflect the change beginning tomorrow, and the ledger would carry the record of that change forward into whatever future the community was given to have.

That was all. That was enough.

After supper, Ruth made her evening rounds. The kitchen was clean, the fires banked, the doors secured. The animals were fed and sheltered for the night. She checked each task, noted each completion, confirmed that everything was as it should be.

She paused in the kitchen doorway before leaving. The room was dark now, the fires reduced to embers, the surfaces wiped and waiting for tomorrow's work. The kettle hung on its hook above the stove, the same kettle that had slipped that morning, the same kettle that Mercy had lifted and carried and used for thirty-one years. Tomorrow, Hannah would lift it. Tomorrow and the next day and the day after that. The kettle would not notice the change. The water would boil regardless of whose hands poured it. The meals would be made, the household would be fed, and the work would continue.

Ruth turned from the kitchen and walked to the assignment board.

She stopped at the assignment board in the hallway and looked at the names she had written that morning, before the kettle, before the conversation, before the adjustment that had changed what the names meant, even though the names themselves remained the same. Tomorrow, she would write new names, new assignments, the schedule reflecting what was now true rather than what had been true yesterday.

She erased the board and began to write.

Sister Mercy: kitchen, supervision. Sister Hannah: kitchen, morning, and afternoon. The chalk moved across the slate, the letters forming in her careful hand, each stroke deliberate and clear. The new arrangement took shape on the board, the new reality made visible in the words that would govern tomorrow's work.

When she finished, she stepped back and looked at what she had written. The board was full. The assignments were complete. Everything was accounted for.

Ruth set down the chalk and wiped her hands on her apron.

CHAPTER EIGHT

Care

Sister Catherine did not come down for the morning meeting.

Ruth noticed her absence the way she noticed all absences. As a fact to be recorded, a variation in the pattern that required acknowledgment, if not immediate response. The women's benches held six instead of seven. The space where Catherine usually sat, third row, nearest the wall, was empty. The meeting proceeded without her, Elder Thomas's voice filling the room with the familiar cadence of morning business, but Ruth's attention kept returning to the empty place, the shape of the person who was not there.

After the meeting, she climbed the stairs to the second floor. The hallway was quiet; the other sisters already dispersed to their morning duties. Catherine's door was closed. Ruth stood before it for a moment, listening. She could hear the cough, the wet, deep sound that had become familiar over the past weeks, but there was something else beneath it, a quality of breathing that sounded effortful in a way it had not sounded before.

She knocked once, softly, and waited.

"Come," Catherine's voice said, and Ruth opened the door.

The room was dim, the curtains still drawn against the morning light. Catherine was sitting on the edge of her bed, not lying down, not standing, but caught somewhere between the two. As if she had meant to rise and had found, partway through the motion, that rising required more than she had expected. Her hands gripped the edge of the mattress. Her feet were flat on the floor, the shoes not yet put on, the stockings still folded on the chair where she had laid them the night before.

"I meant to come down," Catherine said. Her voice was thinner than it had been, worn by the coughing, by the effort of nights that did not provide the rest they were meant to provide. "I woke with the bell. I began dressing. And then." She paused, her breath catching in a way that was not quite a cough. "I found I needed to sit."

Ruth crossed the room and sat in the chair beside the bed. She did not rush. She did not allow alarm to enter her voice or her posture.

"Tell me," Ruth said.

Catherine's hands loosened their grip on the mattress, though they did not leave it entirely. "I stood to dress, as I always stand. I reached for my chemise, as I always reach. And the room." She stopped, searching for the words. "The room was not where I expected it to be. Just for a moment.

Just for the space of a breath. And then it was back, and I was sitting, though I did not remember deciding to sit."

Ruth listened. The words described something she had seen before, in other bodies, in other years. The moment when the flesh announced that it could no longer be taken for granted.

"Has this happened before?" Ruth asked.

"Once. Perhaps twice. I did not think." Catherine's lips pressed together briefly. "I thought it was tiredness. The cough keeps me from sleeping as I should. I thought if I could rest properly, the rest would restore what the cough had taken."

"And the rest has not come."

"No," Catherine said. "The rest has not come."

Ruth looked at Catherine's hands, at the thin fingers that had held a needle for sixty years, that had produced stitches so fine they were nearly invisible. The hands were still capable. She had seen them at work only yesterday. But the hands were attached to a body, and the body was eighty-two years old, and the body was telling a truth that the hands could not contradict.

"You need not come down today," Ruth said. "The meeting has concluded. The morning proceeds. Your absence has been noted, but not as a failure. As rest."

Catherine nodded, but the nod was uncertain. "The mending."

"The mending will wait. Or it will be done by other hands, for a day, while yours recover."

"Hannah is not skilled enough for the fine work."

"Then the fine work will wait until you are ready. There is no deadline that cannot be adjusted."

The room was warming now, the fire that had been banked overnight beginning to release its stored heat. Ruth rose and crossed to the window, drawing the curtains back just enough to let the morning light enter without overwhelming. The light fell across the bed, across Catherine's hands where they still rested on the mattress.

"I will bring you something to eat," Ruth said. "Tea, and bread with butter. You will eat, and then you will rest, and this afternoon we will speak again about what you need."

"I do not wish to be." Catherine stopped.

"To be what?"

"A burden," Catherine said quietly. "Someone who requires attention that could be given elsewhere."

Ruth returned to the chair. "You have given sixty years to this community. Sixty years of skill and patience and labor. If the community now gives you a morning of rest and a meal brought to your room, this is not a burden, this is what we do."

Catherine's eyes were bright. "I have always been the one who cared for others," she said. "I mended their clothes. I taught them to sew. I sat with them when they were ill, and I stitched shrouds when they died. I do not know how to be the one who is cared for."

"Then you will learn," Ruth said. "As you learned everything else."

She rose and moved toward the door. At the threshold, she paused. Catherine had not moved from her position on the edge of the bed, but something in her posture had shifted. A loosening.

"I will return within the hour," Ruth said. "Rest, if you can."

She closed the door and descended the stairs.

For a time, the household moved without correction.

The morning assignments held. No one came to ask for reassignment. Hannah moved from stove to table without pause. Mercy shaped the loaves without faltering. The timing was exact without being counted.

Ruth stood at the threshold and watched. The sound of work filled the spaces between rooms—footsteps, water poured, the soft contact of tools with wood. The house seemed to breathe with them, the work passing through it as naturally as heat.

Nothing required her attention. Nothing needed to be adjusted. She did not reach for her book.

Then the moment passed, as moments did, and the day continued.

Sister Hannah was at the stove when Ruth entered the kitchen, stirring the pot of soup that would be the midday meal. Sister Mercy sat at the work table, her hands sorting through the dried herbs. Hannah no longer looked to Mercy before lifting the heavy kettle. Mercy no longer reached for it herself.

"Sister Catherine will take her breakfast in her room this morning," Ruth said. "I will prepare a tray."

Mercy looked up. "Is she unwell?"

"She is tired. The cough has not eased, and her sleep has suffered. She needs rest more than she needs to be present."

Ruth prepared the tray herself. Tea, bread, butter, and a small bowl of the apple preserves that Catherine had always favored. She arranged the items with care, the cup placed where it could be easily reached, the bread sliced thin enough to be eaten without effort.

She carried the tray up the stairs and knocked again at Catherine's door. When she entered, she found Catherine still sitting on the edge of the bed, but her posture had changed. She was leaning back now, one hand braced against the pillow behind her, as if she had been trying to decide whether to lie down.

"I brought tea," Ruth said. "And something to eat."

She set the tray on the small table and helped Catherine shift her position, arranging the pillows so that she could sit up comfortably. The motions were familiar. Ruth had performed them many times, for many people.

Catherine accepted the tea and held the cup in both hands, letting the warmth seep into her fingers. Her hands were steady, the steadiness of someone whose work had always required precision. But there was a carefulness in the way she held the cup, a wariness that suggested she was aware of how easily things could slip.

"The room feels different," Catherine said, "when one is in it during the hours one is usually elsewhere."

Ruth settled into the chair. She would stay for a few minutes, long enough to ensure that Catherine ate something.

"The light is different," Ruth said. "In the morning, it comes through the east window. You are usually in the sewing room by now, where the light comes from the south."

"Yes." Catherine took a small sip of the tea. "The south light is better for the fine work. I chose that room for the light, years ago. Sister Clarissa wanted the room on the north side, where the light was more even, but I said the brightness was worth the variation. I was right. The stitches show better in bright light."

"You will return to the south light," Ruth said. "When you are rested. When the cough has eased."

"And if the cough does not ease?"

The question was quiet, asked without drama.

"Then we will find another way," Ruth said. "The light can be brought to you if you cannot go to the light. The community adapts. It has always adapted."

Catherine set the teacup down, her hands moving with deliberate care. "I remember when Sister Clarissa could no longer climb the stairs," she said. "We moved her to the room on the first floor, the one with the window that looks out on the garden. She said she did not mind. She said she had climbed enough stairs for one lifetime. But I saw her face, sometimes, when she looked at the staircase. I saw what it cost her to walk past it and know she would not climb it again."

Ruth did not respond immediately. The cost of accommodation, the grief that attended even the kindest adjustments. She had seen that cost many times.

"Sister Clarissa lived three more years after she came downstairs," Ruth said finally. "She finished the altar cloth she had been working on for a decade. She taught four young sisters the techniques she had learned from her own teacher. She died in her sleep, in the room with the garden window, and she was not alone."

"I know," Catherine said. "I was with her."

The silence held.

"You are not Sister Clarissa," Ruth said. "Your body is not her body. Your path may be different."

"Perhaps," Catherine said. "Or perhaps all paths lead to the same place, in the end."

"Perhaps. But we are not at the end. We are here, in this room, on this morning, with tea that is growing cold. The end will come when it comes. Until then, there is this."

Catherine looked at the light that was now fully present through the window. Something in her face eased. Not happiness, exactly, but a kind of acceptance.

"I will eat," Catherine said. "And I will rest. And this afternoon, we will speak again."

"Yes," Ruth said. "This afternoon."

She rose and left the room.

The afternoon brought a conversation with Elder Thomas.

They met in the small room where such conversations always happened. Ruth sat across from him and spoke plainly.

"Sister Catherine's condition concerns me," she said. "Not as emergency, but as change. The cough has not improved. Her strength is less than it was. This morning, she could not rise without difficulty."

Elder Thomas listened without interrupting.

"What do you propose?" he asked when she had finished.

"I propose that Sister Catherine be moved to the room on the first floor," she said. "The room with the garden window. The room where Sister Clarissa spent her final years."

The words hung in the air between them. The room on the first floor was not the infirmary. It was a regular room. But the room had a history, a meaning that attached to it through association. It was where people went when they could no longer manage the stairs.

"The stairs are difficult for her," Ruth continued. "She does not complain, but I have seen her pause at the landing, catching her breath. The cough takes strength she does not have to spare. If she were on the first floor, she would not have to choose between the sewing room and her bed."

"And the sewing room itself?"

"Could remain where it is. Or could be moved to the first floor as well. The work can be done anywhere the light is sufficient."

"You are proposing to bring the work to her, rather than requiring her to go to the work."

"Yes."

"The room is available," Elder Thomas said. "It has been empty since Brother Samuel passed in the spring. It could be ready by tomorrow."

"Tomorrow is soon enough."

"And Sister Catherine's understanding of this change?"

"I have not spoken to her about it directly. I wanted your counsel first. But I believe she will accept it. She has lived long enough to know what the body requires."

Elder Thomas was quiet for a moment. "The room on the first floor carries meaning. Those who have occupied it before—they went there knowing that the stairs they would not climb again were stairs they had climbed for the last time. The room is not confinement. But it is." He paused. "It is completion. The beginning of completion."

"Yes," Ruth said. "I understand."

"And you believe this is appropriate for Sister Catherine? Now, rather than later?"

"I believe the stairs will not become easier. That waiting until the need is undeniable is waiting until the body has been asked to give what it does not have. Better to move while the move is still a kindness."

Elder Thomas nodded. "Then make the arrangements. Speak with Sister Catherine this afternoon. If she is willing, the room can be prepared tonight."

Ruth returned to Catherine's room in the late afternoon. Catherine was awake, sitting up against the pillows, her hands occupied with a small piece of mending that someone had brought to her.

"You see," Catherine said as Ruth entered, "I cannot be idle. Even in bed, the hands must work."

Ruth sat in the chair beside the bed.

"I have spoken with Elder Thomas," Ruth said. "About arrangements that might serve you better."

Catherine's hands paused, the needle suspended mid-stitch.

"There is a room on the first floor," Ruth continued. "The room with the garden window. It is empty now. It is warm and quiet, and does not require climbing stairs. I thought it might suit you better."

Catherine's hands remained still, the mending forgotten.

"The room where Sister Clarissa stayed," Catherine said finally. Her voice was even.

"Yes."

"The room where people go when they cannot manage the stairs."

"The room where people go when the stairs are no longer necessary," Ruth said. "When their work can come to them instead of requiring them to go to it."

Catherine set the mending aside. "I have lived in this room for fifty-one years," she said. "I came here as a girl of thirty-one, and I have slept in this bed ever since. The window faces east. I wake with the sun."

"The garden window faces south. The light will be different. But you will not have to climb stairs that cost more than they should."

"And the sewing room?"

"Will remain where it is, or will be moved to be near you. The work requires only light, a chair, and your hands, which remain capable."

Catherine looked up. "It is kind," she said. "The way you speak of it. Moving the work to me instead of moving me away from the work. Framing it as convenience rather than decline."

"It is not framing," Ruth said. "It is truth. The stairs are difficult. The room is available. The move makes sense."

"And yet more is being said, whether we speak it or not. The room on the first floor is the room where people go at the end. I will know this when I wake in that room tomorrow."

Ruth did not deny it.

"The room is also where people rest," Ruth said. "Where they receive the care they need without having to climb to receive it. Yes, it is the room where endings sometimes begin. But it is also the room where life continues, in whatever form life takes when the stairs are no longer necessary."

Catherine was quiet for a long moment.

"I will go," she said finally. "Tomorrow, if the room is ready. I have lived here long enough to know what it means when the community offers care: it means the care is needed, whether we wish to admit it or not."

"The care is offered," Ruth said gently. "Whether you need it is for your body to say."

Catherine nodded. "I will want to bring the mending. I cannot sit in a room with nothing for my hands to do."

"The mending will come with you. Everything you need will come with you."

"Sister Clarissa brought her altar cloth," Catherine said. "She worked on it until the week before she died. I remember sitting with her, watching her fingers move, thinking how strange it was that hands could work so surely when the body they belonged to was failing."

"Your hands are still sure," Ruth said. "The body may need rest, but the hands know their work."

Catherine looked at the mending, at the neat stitches she had made, at the work that remained to be done.

"Tomorrow," she said. "I will go tomorrow. Tonight I will sleep here one more time, and I will watch the light change through the east window one more time. And tomorrow I will learn to wake with a different light."

"Tomorrow," Ruth agreed. She stood and crossed to the door. "I will have the room prepared tonight. The fire will be lit. The bed will be made. And you will have only to walk down the stairs one more time."

She closed the door and descended the stairs.

That evening, Ruth supervised the preparation of the room on the first floor. The linens were aired and freshened. The fire was laid and lit, the warmth beginning to build against the November cold. The furniture was arranged. The bed positioned where the light from the garden window would fall across it in the morning, the chair placed near the window for sitting, the small table set within reach of both.

Before retiring, she climbed the stairs one more time to bring Catherine her evening tray. Tea, a bowl of broth, bread that had been softened in the warming oven.

She knocked and entered. The room was dim, the fire burning low. Catherine sat in the chair by the window, not in bed, looking out at the darkness that had settled over the yard.

"I brought your supper," Ruth said.

Catherine did not turn. "Thank you. You can set it on the table."

Ruth crossed the room and placed the tray where Catherine could reach it. She straightened and was about to leave when she noticed Catherine's hands.

They rested in her lap, the mending set aside, the needle nowhere in sight. But the hands were not still. The fingers were moving. Slightly, almost imperceptibly, a small motion that Catherine herself did not seem to notice.

Ruth watched. The motion was not sewing. The fingers were not guiding an invisible needle, not pulling invisible thread. The motion was something else. The hands were shaping something. Tracing something. Moving in a pattern that had no name, Ruth could give it a rhythm that belonged to no work she had ever seen Catherine do.

The fingers curved and opened, curved and opened. As if molding air. As if remembering a gesture the body had once known how to make, something the hands had done long ago, before the needle, before the thread, before the sixty years of stitches that had defined Catherine's contribution to this place.

Ruth thought of the floors. The circles worn into the wood in the small room off the hall. The chaotic patterns in the children's dormitory. The arcs in the meeting hall that had nothing to do with walking or sitting.

Catherine's fingers curved and opened. Curved and opened. The motion small and steady, unconscious. Her face was turned toward the window, toward the darkness, seeing nothing of what her hands were doing.

Ruth looked away.

"Is there anything else you need?" she asked. Her voice was steady.

Catherine turned from the window. Her hands stilled in her lap, the motion ceasing as her attention shifted. She looked at the tray, at the broth, at the bread, at the tea that was still warm.

"No," she said. "Everything I need is here."

Ruth nodded and moved toward the door.

"Sleep well," she said. "Tomorrow will be a new beginning."

"Yes," Catherine said. "It will."

Ruth closed the door and descended the stairs.

She did not go to her room.

Instead, she walked to the first floor, to the room with the garden window, to the space that had been prepared for the person who would occupy it tomorrow.

The fire was burning steadily. The bed was made, the linens fresh, the pillows arranged for comfort. The chair waited by the window. The small table held nothing yet—tomorrow it would hold Catherine's mending, her tea, the objects that would make the room hers.

Ruth stood in the doorway and looked at the room.

The floorboards here were worn too. Not in circles, not in the patterns of ecstatic movement, but in the path between the bed and the window, the bed and the door. The path of someone who had lived within these walls, who had walked from rest to light and back again, day after day, until the walking stopped.

Tomorrow, Catherine would begin wearing her own path into this floor. Tomorrow her feet would trace the route from bed to window, from window to chair, from chair to wherever the mending waited. The path would deepen over time—weeks, months, however long the body continued its work of continuing.

The room was ready. The fire crackled. The warmth built against the November cold.

Ruth stepped inside and closed the door behind her.

She crossed to the window and looked out at the garden, visible only as shapes in the darkness, the beds where nothing grew now, the paths that would not be walked until spring. Catherine would see this view every morning. Catherine would watch the garden return to life, or she would not. The room did not know. The room only waited.

Ruth turned back to face the space. The bed, the chair, the fire, the careful arrangement of comfort. Everything ready. Everything prepared.

Tomorrow, the room would hold a person. Tonight it held only the readiness, the anticipation, the particular silence of a space that knew what it was for.

Ruth stood in that silence for a long moment.

Then she crossed to the fire and checked that the damper was set correctly, that the warmth would last through the night, that everything was as it should be.

She left the room and closed the door behind her.

The hallway was quiet. The household was asleep. Behind one door, Catherine was spending her last night in the room with the east window, her hands perhaps still moving in patterns she did not see.

Ruth walked to her own room and prepared for bed.

But the image that stayed with her as she closed her eyes was not Catherine's hands, and not the stairs that would be descended one final time.

It was the room. The garden window. The fire burning steadily in the darkness.

The space, waiting to receive what the stairs could no longer carry.

CHAPTER NINE

Doctrine

The morning meeting began with a reading.

This was not unusual. The meetings often began this way, with Elder Thomas's voice carrying the words that had been written long ago, words that had been read in this room for generations. The household sat in their usual places, the women on one side, the men on the other, the arrangement unchanged from how it had been for a hundred years. The light came through the eastern windows as it always came, falling across the polished floor in long rectangles that shifted imperceptibly as the sun rose.

Ruth sat in her usual seat and listened.

"We are called to be faithful stewards of what we are given," Elder Thomas read. His voice was steady, unhurried, the voice of someone who had read these words many times and would read them many times more. "The body is given to us for a season. We do not own it; we tend it. When the season changes, we must change with it."

The words were from the early writings, the testimonies that had been collected and preserved from the time of Mother Ann herself. Ruth had heard them before. Everyone had heard them before. But this morning something moved beneath the familiar surface, something she had not noticed in the hundred times she had heard these passages read.

The people who first spoke these words had felt seasons pass through them. They had danced until they fell. They had risen again changed. The words were not comfort; they were testimony—descriptions of what had happened to real bodies in real rooms. The experience had become text, and the text had become doctrine, and the doctrine had become the smooth phrases Elder Thomas spoke each morning in his measured voice.

Ruth heard the words differently now. She heard what was beneath them.

"To resist the body's wisdom," Elder Thomas continued, "is to resist the wisdom that made it."

His voice caught.

It was slight. Almost imperceptible. A hesitation between one word and the next, a breath held half a beat longer than the rhythm required. Ruth watched him. She had been watching without intention, her eyes resting on his face as her ears received the words, but now she watched with attention.

Elder Thomas's eyes had closed. Not in the way eyes close for a blink, quickly and without thought. They closed and remained closed, the lids lowered over whatever was happening behind them, the pause stretching for one breath, then two.

Something moved across his face.

Ruth could not name it. It was not pain. It was not grief. It was something older than either, something that had been held for so long that holding it had become invisible, and now, for just this moment, the holding was visible.

Then his eyes opened. His voice resumed. The rhythm restored itself.

"The harvest is not less faithful than the planting. The rest is not less holy than the labor."

The words continued as if nothing had happened. Elder Thomas read them as he always read them, steady and unhurried, the voice of a man who had performed this service for forty years and would perform it as long as he was able.

But Ruth had seen.

She had seen his eyes close. She had seen something move across his face that he had not permitted to move there in all the years she had known him. And she understood, suddenly, what she had not understood before.

Elder Thomas remembered.

He was seventy-four years old. He had come to this community as a young man of twenty-three in 1846. And in those early years, when he was new and the community was different, he had seen bodies shake and the gift descend.

He had been young when the fires were still burning. He had seen the furnace before it was banked.

And he had chosen not to speak of it. Not because speaking was forbidden, but because speaking would be mourning, or longing, or the admission that what they had now was not what they had once had.

He carried the memory the way the walls carried the memory of the dancing, the way the floors carried the wear of feet that had moved in patterns no one moved in anymore.

The reading continued.

Ruth sat in the silence of her own recognition and let the words wash over her. The harvest is not less faithful than the planting. The rest is not less holy than the labor. The words were what remained—what could be spoken now without waking the floors.

Catherine was not present at the meeting.

This was expected. The room on the first floor was closer to everything that mattered. The kitchen, the common areas, the warmth of the central fires. But it was not closer to the meeting room. Catherine would take her meals in her new room, at least for now. She would rest when rest was needed. She would work when work was possible.

Elder Thomas closed the book. The sound was soft. Leather against leather, the pages settling. But it carried through the quiet room.

"Sister Catherine has moved to the room on the first floor," Elder Thomas said. This was not announcement; it was acknowledgment. The household already knew. "She will continue her work as she is able. We will attend to her needs as the community has always attended to the needs of its members. This is not change; this is faithfulness. This is what we have always done."

The words were simple, practical, requiring no response. Ruth heard them and felt something loosen in her chest.

But she also heard what was beneath the words now. She heard the echo of older words, words that had been spoken when faithfulness meant something different, when attending to a body's needs might have meant making space for the spirit to move through it, not simply keeping it warm and fed while it declined.

The meeting ended with silence, as meetings always ended. Ruth sat in the silence and let it hold her. She watched Elder Thomas, whose eyes were open now, whose face had returned to its usual patient composure.

Then the silence ended, and the day began.

She visited Catherine after breakfast.

The room with the garden window was warm, the fire built up against the November cold, the light falling through the glass in the particular way that south-facing windows allowed. Catherine was seated in the chair by the window, her hands occupied with the mending she had brought from her old room, the needle moving through fabric with the same precision it had always shown.

"The light is different," Catherine said. "But it is good light. I can see the stitches clearly."

Ruth pulled the other chair closer and sat.

"Elder Thomas read from the early testimonies this morning," Ruth said. "The passage about the body's seasons."

Catherine nodded. Her hands did not pause in their work. "I know that passage. I have heard it many times. 'The harvest is not less faithful than the planting.'" She smiled slightly. "It is a good passage for a morning like this one."

"It is."

"I did not sleep well last night," Catherine said. "The room was unfamiliar. The sounds were different. I kept waking, expecting to see the east window, expecting the light to come from a direction it would not come from anymore." She paused, the needle stilling for a moment before resuming. "But this morning I woke with the sun on my face, and I thought: this is the light I will learn. This is the season I am in now. And the passage." She shook her head slightly. "It is strange how words you have heard a hundred times can suddenly mean something new."

Ruth understood. She had felt it herself, in the meeting room, when the familiar words had opened and shown her what was beneath them.

"Is there anything you need?" Ruth asked. "Anything that would make the room more comfortable?"

"No," Catherine said. "Everything I need is here. The mending. The fire. The light." She looked toward the window, toward the garden that was dormant now but would bloom again in spring. "And the window. I can see the garden from here. I never thought about the garden much when I was upstairs. It was just there, outside, something I passed on my way to other places. But now I will watch it. I will see it change through the seasons. There is something." She paused. "Something complete about that. Watching one thing change while I change alongside it."

She was quiet for a moment, her hands still moving through the fabric.

"Sister Clarissa told me once that the garden window was a kindness," Catherine said. "She said that by the time you can see the garden from inside, you have stopped needing to walk in it."

The words hung in the air. Ruth did not respond. There was nothing to say that the words had not already said.

"The physician will come tomorrow," Ruth said finally. "To check on the cough."

"The cough will do what it will do," Catherine said. "The physician is kind, and his remedies are useful. But I have lived in this body for eighty-two years. I know what it is telling me. The cough is not the illness; it is the body speaking. And I am learning to listen."

Ruth rose to leave. At the door, she paused and looked back. Catherine had returned to her mending, her hands moving with their accustomed sureness. The light from the garden window fell across her work, illuminating the stitches.

"I will check on you this afternoon," Ruth said.

"Someone always does," Catherine said. She did not look up.

Ruth closed the door and stood for a moment in the hallway.

The reading had done its work. But it had also shown her what lay beneath the work. Elder Thomas remembered. His eyes had closed, and something had moved across his face, and Ruth had seen it.

She did not know what to do with what she had seen. There was nothing to do with it. The seeing changed nothing. The practice continued.

But now she knew that the words had once meant something else. And the person reading them knew it too.

She returned to her duties.

The afternoon brought a conversation with Sister Eunice.

They met in the herb drying shed, where Eunice was arranging the last of the autumn's harvest on the racks. The air was warm and fragrant, thick with the smell of sage and thyme and chamomile. Eunice's hands moved through the dried stems with the efficiency of practice, her attention divided between the work before her and Ruth's presence at the doorway.

"I heard about Sister Catherine," Eunice said. "The room on the first floor."

Ruth stepped into the shed. "The arrangement was necessary. The stairs were difficult. The cough takes strength she does not have to spare."

"I understand." Eunice's hands did not pause. "I saw her yesterday, before the move. She looked tired. More tired than usual. The kind of tired that does not improve with a single night's sleep."

"Yes."

"Is she?" Eunice stopped, her hands stilling. "Will she recover? From the cough, from the tiredness? Will the room on the first floor be temporary, or."

She did not finish the question.

Ruth considered her answer carefully. "The room is the right place for her now. Whether it is temporary or permanent is not for us to decide. We care for her today. Tomorrow we will care for her again. The body has its seasons, and we attend to each season as it comes. That is what faithfulness means."

Eunice nodded slowly. Her hands resumed their work. "I know. I know all of that. It's just..." She shook her head. "I think about my own hands sometimes. How they still work. How they might not always work. I think about the garden, and what will happen to it when I am not able to tend it. Who will know which plants to harvest first? Who will know how long to dry the chamomile before it loses its strength?"

"Someone will learn," Ruth said. "As you learned. As everyone has learned. The knowledge passes from hand to hand. That is how it has always been."

"But there are fewer hands now." Eunice's voice was quiet. "When I came here, there were three of us in the garden. Then two. Now one." She picked up a stem of boneset, turned it in her fingers. "The boneset has to be harvested the morning the first flowers open. Not before, not after. One day. Sister Margaret taught me that. She could tell by the smell when it was ready, before she could even see the blossoms. I learned to smell it too. But if I don't teach someone else." She set the stem down. "Who will know? Who will smell it?"

The question hung in the air, mixed with the scent of the drying herbs.

"We do what we can," Ruth said. "We teach what we know. We pass on what we have received. And when we can no longer do or teach or pass on, we trust that what was meant to continue will continue, and what was meant to complete will complete. That is the covenant."

Eunice was quiet for a long moment.

"I confessed this, you know," Eunice said finally. "The resentment. The worry about the garden. I confessed it on Thursday, and Elder Thomas listened, and he said what he always says. That the worry is human, that confessing it releases its power, that I can return to the work without carrying what I carried before." She looked up, her eyes meeting Ruth's. "And it helped. It always helps. But sometimes I think." She stopped. "I don't know what I think. The confession clears the weight, but the weight returns. And I confess again, and it clears again. And I wonder if the clearing is really clearing, or if it's just. Moving things from one place to another. Rearranging the worry instead of removing it."

Ruth heard the words. She thought of Elder Thomas's eyes closing, of what had moved across his face.

"The confession is for the soul," Ruth said. "The worry is for the body. They are not the same. The soul can be clear even when the body remains troubled. That is part of what it means to live in flesh that has not yet been perfected."

Eunice nodded slowly. The tension in her shoulders eased slightly. "I know. I know all of that. Sometimes I just need to hear it again."

"That is why we read the testimonies every morning," Ruth said. "Not because we have forgotten, but because we need to be reminded. The reminding is part of the practice."

Even as she said the words, she thought of what she had heard beneath them that morning. The reminding was part of the practice. But the practice had changed.

Eunice returned to her work. Ruth watched her for a moment, then turned and left the shed, stepping out into the cold air of the November afternoon.

Supper was quiet, as supper always was.

The household gathered around the long table, the food passed in the usual order, the silence held except for the small necessary words.

Partway through the meal, Sister Mercy said something to Hannah about the morning's reading. Ruth did not hear the words clearly. They were spoken softly, meant only for the two of them. But she saw Hannah nod in response. The nod was simple, untroubled, the acknowledgment of something that required no discussion.

Ruth watched her for a moment longer. Hannah was thirty-five years old. She had come to the community at twenty-three, had learned its ways, and had absorbed its teachings. The reading that morning had settled something in Ruth. It had confirmed something for Catherine. It had met Eunice's worry with an answer that cleared the weight, at least for now.

But Hannah had simply nodded. The reading had required nothing of her. She was already inside what Ruth had needed the reading to restore.

And Elder Thomas had closed his eyes and held something that Hannah would never need to hold, because Hannah had never seen what Elder Thomas had seen.

Ruth returned to her meal. The silence continued.

That evening, after supper, Ruth sat in the small office and opened the ledger.

The pages were familiar. The columns of names, the rows of tasks, the careful notations that tracked every assignment and every change. She turned to the page where Catherine's name appeared and looked at what she had written: the new room, the new arrangement.

She added a note in the margin, small and precise: "Nov. 24 — Reading: Body's seasons."

It was not standard practice to note such things. The ledger was for practical matters. Who was assigned where, what work was being done, what supplies were needed. It was not for recording which passages had been read or which teachings had been invoked.

But Ruth wrote the note anyway. The reading was part of the arrangement in a way that the practical notations alone could not capture. The decision to move Catherine had been made for practical reasons—the stairs, the cough, the difficulty. But the reading had given it a place within the framework of belief, had transformed it from a practical necessity into an act of faithfulness.

She thought of Elder Thomas reading the words. His voice catching. His eyes closing.

He had transformed a practical necessity into an act of faithfulness too. Every morning for forty years, he had read words that once described things he had seen with his own eyes, and he had made those words serve a different purpose now, a quieter purpose.

The words still worked. They worked for Catherine. They worked for Eunice. They worked for Ruth herself.

But they worked differently now than they had worked when they were first spoken. And Elder Thomas knew the difference. And he read them anyway, his eyes closing sometimes, something moving across his face that he did not permit to be spoken.

That was faithfulness too. A different kind.

Ruth closed the ledger.

She rose and left the office, walking through the darkening hallway toward her room.

She passed the door to Catherine's new room on the first floor. Light showed beneath the door. The lamp lit, the fire burning, the room inhabited. She paused for a moment, listening. No coughing, no movement, no sound at all. Just the quiet presence of someone at rest, someone being cared for.

She continued to her room and prepared for bed.

The sequence was familiar, automatic. Undressing, folding, the brief prayers that had been spoken every night for forty-three years. The prayers asked for guidance, for strength, for faithfulness. The prayers did not ask for understanding.

Ruth climbed into bed.

The sheets were cool, then warm. The house was quiet around her.

Across the room, Abigail's breathing was already slow and even. She had heard the same reading that morning. She had not needed to discuss it with anyone.

Ruth thought about the words that had been spoken, the words that had settled the uncertainty she had carried.

The body has its seasons. The harvest is not less faithful than the planting. We do not cling to what passes.

The words moved through her mind like water, like breath. They were the words that made everything else possible. The care, the arrangement, the smooth continuation of a community that had been caring for its members in exactly this way for a hundred years.

The words were not new. They would never be new. That was their power.

But this morning, Ruth had heard what was beneath them. She had seen Elder Thomas's eyes close. She had understood that the words had once described something that some of them still remembered, something they carried in silence.

The silence was its own kind of speech.

Ruth closed her eyes.

The words would be read again tomorrow, and the day after, and the day after that. They would do their work, and the work would be good.

Nothing had changed. Everything had been confirmed.

Ruth slept.

And somewhere in the house, Elder Thomas slept too, holding what he held, carrying what he carried, his eyes closed over whatever moved behind them when the words he read reminded him of things he had seen when the words were not yet words but the names of what was happening all around him, in bodies that shook and voices that spoke and a spirit that moved through receptive hearts like fire.

The fire had banked. The order remained.

The holding continued.

CHAPTER TEN

Labor

Hannah was at the stove when Ruth arrived. The fire had been burning for an hour.

She was stirring the oats that would be the morning's breakfast, her movements steady and unhurried. Sister Mercy sat at the work table, her hands sorting through the dried beans that would become the afternoon's soup, separating the whole from the broken with the efficiency of long practice. The fire had been built up against the November cold, the wood stacked and burning in the particular way that produced heat without waste.

This was how it was done now.

Ruth stood in the doorway and watched for a moment, as she often watched when she arrived before the others. The rhythm of the kitchen had changed over the past weeks. Not dramatically, not in any way that would have been visible to someone seeing it for the first time, but perceptibly to someone who had observed it for years. Hannah moved with more certainty now, her hands reaching for tools and ingredients without looking, her body knowing the space in the way that only primary responsibility could teach. Mercy's movements were slower, more deliberate, her attention focused on the tasks that required precision rather than strength.

The work was being done. The work was always being done. Only the distribution had shifted, the weight settling differently across the available hands.

Ruth entered the kitchen and began her morning inspection. The bread was rising in its covered bowls, the yeast doing its patient work. The preserves were stocked, the dried herbs hung in their proper bundles, the root vegetables stored in the cold cellar where they would keep through the winter. She checked each station without comment, noting what was present and what would need replenishment, her mind already calculating the tasks that the day would require.

"The flour is running low," Hannah said without looking up from the oats. "I've measured what remains. Four days, perhaps five, before we need to grind more."

"I will note it," Ruth said. "Brother Thomas can manage the mill tomorrow, if his back permits."

"And if it does not?"

The question was practical, not anxious. Hannah was learning to think this way. To see beyond the immediate task to the dependencies that surrounded it, the chain of hands and capacities that made any single piece of work possible.

"Then we will manage," Ruth said. "We always manage."

She left the kitchen and continued through the stations.

The workshop was her next stop. The long building set apart from the dwellings, where the furniture was made that brought income to the community and reputation to its craftsmen. Brother Daniel was at his bench, as he always was, his hands moving over a piece of cherry wood with the sureness that fifty years of practice had given him. Brother William worked at the smaller bench near the window, his movements careful, considered, still learning what Daniel had spent decades perfecting.

But it was Brother James who drew Ruth's attention this morning.

James was sixty-seven years old. He had worked in the workshop for forty-three years, not as a furniture maker but as a tool keeper, a sharpener, a mender of the instruments that made the finer work possible. His hands had always been steady. The sharpening of planes and chisels required steadiness. The setting of saw teeth required precision. The work was not glamorous, but it was essential. Without sharp tools, no furniture could be made. Without James's maintenance, Daniel's artistry would have no instruments through which to express itself.

This morning, James stood at the grinding wheel, a chisel in his hand, attempting to restore the edge that use had dulled.

Ruth watched from the doorway as his hands positioned the blade against the stone.

The hands were shaking.

Not dramatically. Not in the way that would have been immediately visible to someone not watching closely. But Ruth was watching closely, and she saw the tremor. The small vibration that made the blade waver against the wheel, that made the angle uncertain, that turned what should have been automatic into something requiring conscious effort and constant correction.

James adjusted his grip. The tremor continued. He pressed the blade more firmly against the stone, trying to steady it through pressure, but the pressure only made the shaking more visible, the effort of control now apparent in the tension of his arms, his shoulders, his jaw.

The chisel in his hand was old. Ruth could see the wear on the handle, the patina that decades of use had given the wood. She knew this chisel. She had seen it in Brother Samuel's hands, years ago, when Samuel was still alive and still working. Samuel had made this chisel himself, in 1847, forging the blade and fitting the handle in the workshop that was now occupied by men who had learned from men who had learned from him.

Samuel had made tools with the precision of prayer. Ruth remembered this now, watching James struggle with the chisel Samuel had made. The making had been prayer.

Samuel had spoken of it once, years ago, in the way that the older members sometimes spoke of things that younger members did not fully understand. He had said that the designs came to him in meeting. That he would sit in the silence, his hands folded, his heart open, and the shape of what he should make would appear in his mind. Not chosen. Given.

James set the chisel down. His hands rested on the workbench, the tremor still visible, the effort of the morning already exhausting him. He did not look up. He did not need to look up to know that Ruth was watching.

"The edge is not right," he said. His voice was quiet, matter-of-fact. "I will try again this afternoon. Sometimes the hands are better in the afternoon."

Ruth did not respond. There was nothing to say. The hands would be what the hands would be. The afternoon might be better, or it might not. The chisel would be sharpened eventually, by James or by someone else, and the work would continue.

But the chisel would outlast him. Samuel's chisel, made in 1847, would still be here when James's hands could no longer hold it. The tool would pass to other hands, hands that had never known Samuel, hands that would not know that the making had been prayer.

Ruth left the workshop without speaking.

The laundry shed was cold, the fires not yet built for the day's work. Sister Eunice was there already, sorting the linens that had accumulated over the week, her hands moving through the fabric with the same efficiency she brought to the herb garden. The great copper kettles stood empty, waiting for the water that would be carried from the well, the lye that would be mixed, and the labor that would transform soiled cloth into clean.

"The lye needs checking," Eunice said as Ruth entered. "I mixed a new batch yesterday, but I am not certain of the strength."

Ruth crossed to where the lye water stood in its wooden barrel, the pale liquid still and waiting. She knew what Eunice meant. The strength of the lye was not something that could be measured with instruments or written in recipes. It was something learned through years of practice, through the particular sting against the skin, through the smell that indicated readiness without ever being quite describable.

Sister Agnes had known the lye by smell alone. She could stand at the barrel's edge, breathe in once, and say with certainty whether the water was ready or whether it needed another day, another measure of ash, another turning. She had tried to teach this knowledge to the younger sisters, had stood beside them at the barrel and described what she sensed, but description was not transmission. The knowledge lived in Agnes's body, in the particular configuration of her senses that decades of practice had refined, and when Agnes died three winters ago, that knowledge had died with her.

Eunice had learned what she could. She checked the lye by touch now, by the feel of it against her fingers, by the way it changed the texture of a scrap of cloth dipped into the barrel. Her method worked. The laundry was done, and the linens were clean. But it was slower, less certain, requiring tests where Agnes had required only breath.

"It seems ready," Eunice said. "But I would value your judgment."

Ruth dipped her own fingers into the barrel, felt the familiar sting, and rubbed the liquid between thumb and forefinger. The lye was strong enough. The work could proceed.

"It will serve," she said. "Begin when you are ready."

She left the laundry shed and continued through the stations.

The sewing room was warm, the fire built up against the cold, the south-facing windows admitting the thin November light. But the room was empty. The chairs stood waiting, the work baskets arranged in their usual places, the half-finished mending folded neatly on the central table. Catherine was no longer here.

Ruth stood in the doorway for a moment, looking at the space that Catherine had occupied for sixty years. The room still held the shape of her presence. The particular chair she had preferred positioned near the window where the light fell strongest. The small table beside it where she had kept her finest needles. The worn spot on the floor where her feet had rested through thousands of hours of careful stitching.

But Catherine was on the first floor now, in the room with the garden window, and the sewing room waited for someone to fill what she had left.

Hannah came here in the afternoons, when the kitchen work was done. She sat in a different chair, used different needles, brought a different quality of attention to the mending that accumulated. Her stitches were adequate. Neat, functional, sufficient for the repairs that daily use required. But they were not Catherine's stitches, and the fine work, the delicate seams, the invisible joins, the repairs that restored fabric to something better than mere functionality, the fine work waited in a basket by the window, accumulating.

Ruth crossed to the basket and looked at what it held. A torn lace collar that had belonged to Sister Agnes, saved for repair but not yet repaired. A silk ribbon, frayed at the edges, that had been used for decades in the celebration of particular holy days. A woolen shawl with a seam that had begun to separate, the original stitching too fine to be replicated by hands that had not learned the technique.

The basket was fuller than it had been the week before.

Ruth left the sewing room and descended the stairs to the first floor.

Catherine was in her chair by the garden window, her lap covered with a cloth on which she had spread an assortment of threads. She was sorting them by color and weight, her fingers moving through the tangled skeins with patient attention, separating what could be separated and setting aside what was too knotted to save. The work was quiet, small, requiring attention but not strength.

"Good morning," Ruth said from the doorway.

Catherine looked up. Her face was calm, her expression the settled composure that had characterized her since the move to this room. "Good morning. I am making order from disorder." She gestured at the threads. "Someone brought me the remnants from the sewing room. Years of accumulated ends and tangles. I am sorting what can still be used."

Ruth entered and sat in the chair across from Catherine, watching her hands move through the threads. The fingers were thin now, the joints more prominent than they had been, but they moved with precision, finding the beginning of each tangle, working it loose with patient manipulation.

"This green," Catherine said, holding up a length of thread, "is from the batch we dyed in '89. I remember the color. We used walnut hulls with iron, and the green came out darker than we intended. Sister Patience said it looked like the bottom of a pond." She smiled slightly. "I have always liked it."

"Will it be used again?"

"Perhaps. If someone needs a dark green thread for mending. If the mending requires thread of this weight." Catherine set the green thread aside, in a small pile with others of similar hue. "The work is small. But it is work."

Ruth heard the words and understood what lay beneath them. The work is small. But it is work. As long as there was work, there was place. As long as the hands could contribute something, even something as modest as sorted thread, the person attached to those hands remained part of the pattern, woven into the fabric of the community's daily life.

"The fine mending accumulates," Ruth said. "In the sewing room. Hannah does what she can, but."

"But Hannah did not learn the fine stitches," Catherine said. "I know. I should have taught her years ago, when my hands were still quick enough to demonstrate. Now I can describe, but description is not the same as showing. She tries. The trying is faithful. But the stitches are not the same."

"Could you teach her still? From here, with words, with guidance?"

Catherine was quiet for a moment, her hands still moving through the threads, finding and sorting, finding and sorting. "I have tried," she said. "She comes in the afternoons, sometimes, and I tell her how the needle should move, where the thread should enter, how tight the tension should be. She listens. She practices. But." Catherine shook her head. "The fine stitches are not learned through listening. They are learned through the hand holding the hand, through the feeling of the right movement passing from one body to another. I cannot hold her hand now. My hand is not steady enough. So I describe, and she tries, and the stitches are better than they were, but not what they should be."

The words were not a complaint. They were observation, the clear-eyed recognition of a limit that could not be overcome through effort or intention. Catherine saw what was true and named it without bitterness, without protest, without any expectation that naming would change what was named.

"Some knowledge passes," Ruth said. "Some does not."

"Yes," Catherine said. "That is the nature of things. We do not choose what survives."

Ruth rose to leave. At the door, she paused and looked back. Catherine had returned to her sorting, her head bent over the threads, her fingers patient and precise. The light from the garden window fell across her work, illuminating the colors, making visible the small contributions that remained possible.

"I will check on you this afternoon," Ruth said.

"I will be here," Catherine said. "I am always here now."

Ruth returned to the kitchen for the midday meal.

The household gathered around the long table, the food served in the usual order, the silence held except for the necessary words. Ruth ate and watched. The faces around the table were familiar. Mercy, Hannah, Martha, Eunice, the brothers on their side, Elder Thomas at the head. Twelve people where there had once been thirty. Twelve hands where there had once been sixty.

The food was sufficient. The meal was adequate. The work had been done.

After the meal, Ruth helped clear the dishes, carrying them to the kitchen where Hannah had already begun the washing. The work was routine, the movements automatic, the kind of labor that required hands but not thought. Ruth dried the dishes as Hannah washed them, the rhythm familiar, the silence comfortable.

"Sister Mercy spoke to me this morning," Hannah said, her hands still moving through the soapy water. "She asked if I could take over the early bread preparation. She said her hands are too stiff in the cold mornings to manage the kneading as quickly as it requires."

Ruth continued drying, her movements unchanged. "And what did you say?"

"I said yes. Of course I said yes. She has taught me the bread. I can manage it."

"Good."

The conversation ended. The dishes were finished. Hannah drained the water and wiped down the surfaces while Ruth returned the dried dishes to their places on the shelves. The kitchen was clean, the work complete, the afternoon's tasks waiting to begin.

Ruth left the kitchen and went to find Mercy.

She found her in the hallway outside the kitchen, standing by the window that looked out on the garden. Mercy's hands were folded in front of her, her posture still, her attention fixed on something Ruth could not see. The dormant plants, perhaps, or the frost on the glass, or nothing at all.

"Sister Mercy," Ruth said.

Mercy turned. Her face was calm, her expression the neutral composure that years in the community had cultivated. "Sister Ruth. I was waiting for you. I thought you might come."

"Hannah told me about the bread."

"Yes." Mercy looked down at her hands, at the fingers that had kneaded and shaped and formed for thirty-one years. "I should have spoken to you first. Before asking Hannah. That would have been the proper order."

"The order does not matter. The work matters. If Hannah can do the bread, then Hannah should do the bread."

Mercy nodded, but she did not look up. Her hands remained folded, the fingers still, the joints swollen in the way that cold weather made worse. "I am sorry," she said quietly. "For being slower. For needing to ask for help. I know that the work does not wait for my hands to remember how to move."

The apology hung in the air between them. Small, practical, offered without drama or self-pity. An apology for pace, for timing, for the failure of flesh to perform what it had always performed. An apology for being less than she had been.

Ruth heard it. She let it stand.

"The bread will be made," Ruth said. "That is what matters."

"Yes," Mercy said. "The bread will be made."

She did not say: but not by me, not anymore. She did not need to say it. The words had already done their work, had already drawn the line that separated what Mercy had been from what she now was.

Ruth returned to her duties.

The afternoon passed in the usual sequence of tasks. Ruth checked the stores in the cellar, noting what would need replenishment before winter deepened. She consulted with Elder Thomas about the mill, about Brother Thomas's back, about the work that would need to be done before the first heavy snow. She observed the laundry shed, where Eunice had begun the washing, the lye water doing its work on the soiled linens, the steam rising in the cold air.

She returned to the workshop in the late afternoon. Brother Daniel was still at his bench, the cherry wood taking shape under his hands, the furniture that would bring income to the community emerging slowly from the raw material. Brother William worked beside him, his movements still careful, still learning.

Brother James was at the grinding wheel again. His hands held a different tool now, a plane blade that needed sharpening. Ruth watched from the doorway as he positioned the blade against the stone.

The tremor was still there. But James had found a way to manage it. He braced his wrist against the edge of the wheel's housing, using the structure to steady what his muscles could no longer steady on their own. The blade moved against the stone with something approaching evenness. Not the fluid motion it would have had in younger hands. But adequate. Sufficient. The edge would be restored. The work would be done.

Ruth watched him for a moment longer, then turned and continued through the stations.

She found Brother Thomas at the woodshed, stacking the logs that would be needed for the evening fires. His movements were careful, deliberate, the movements of someone whose body required more attention than it once had. He was sixty-eight years old, and he had been doing this work, cutting, splitting, stacking, for thirty-one years. His arms were still strong, but his back had begun to betray him, and the lifting that had once been automatic now required calculation.

"The oak is well seasoned," he said when Ruth approached. "It will burn clean through January."

"And after January?"

"The maple will be ready. I have stacked it where it will dry." He set another log in place, his hands finding the position by habit, by the accumulated knowledge of decades. "Brother Samuel used to help with the heavy lifting. Since his passing, the work takes longer."

Ruth nodded. Brother Samuel had died in the spring, quietly, in the room on the first floor that Catherine now occupied. He had been the last of the brothers who could still manage the sustained physical labor that winter required. Now there was only Brother Thomas, and Elder Thomas, and Brother William, who was eighty-four and could no longer lift anything heavier than a book.

"I manage," Brother Thomas said. "The wood will be stacked. The fires will burn."

"Yes," Ruth said. "The fires will burn."

She continued through the stations, moving through the buildings, checking what had been done and what remained to be done. Everywhere she looked, she saw the same pattern: the same names appearing again and again, the same hands absorbing what other hands had released. Hannah in the kitchen and the sewing room. Eunice in the garden and the laundry. Brother Thomas at the woodshed, alone now where there had been two. James was at the grinding wheel, bracing his wrist to steady the tremor.

In the early evening, she returned to the small office and opened the ledger.

The pages were familiar. The columns of names, the rows of tasks, the careful notations that tracked every assignment and every change. She turned to the current week's entries and looked at what she had written over the past days. Hannah's name appeared seven times. Eunice's name appeared five. Mercy's name, which had once filled entire columns, appeared twice, and both entries were for tasks that required judgment rather than labor. Oversight, guidance, supervision.

Ruth added the day's changes: Hannah taking the morning bread. Small adjustments, reasonable accommodations, the kind of shifts that any well-managed household would make when circumstances required. Nothing dramatic. Nothing alarming. Simply the ongoing work of fitting available hands to necessary tasks.

She turned back through the ledger, looking at the entries from a month ago, from six months ago, from a year. The pattern was clear to anyone who knew how to read it. Fewer names appearing more frequently. The same hands doing more kinds of work. The specialized knowledge that had once been distributed across many people now concentrated in fewer, and some of that knowledge, like Agnes's sense for the lye, like Catherine's fine stitches, like

Samuel's prayerful toolmaking, not concentrated anywhere at all, but simply absent, the space it had occupied now empty.

Ruth closed the ledger and sat for a moment in the quiet office.

She rose from the desk and left the office.

The evening meal was quiet, as evening meals always were. The household gathered, the food was served, the silence held. Ruth ate and watched. The faces around the table showed nothing unusual. Tiredness, perhaps, the ordinary weariness that came at the end of a day's work, but nothing that would have seemed remarkable to an outside observer. The community was fed. The community was functioning. The day was drawing to its close.

After the meal, Ruth completed her evening circuit. The kitchen was clean, the fires banked, the doors secured. The laundry was finished, the linens hung to dry in the heated space where they would be ready for folding in the morning.

She checked each station, noted each completion, confirmed that everything was as it should be. The work had been done. The work was always done.

At the woodshed, she paused. Brother Thomas had stacked the logs for tomorrow, but the splitting block still held the axe, left where he had set it when his back had required him to stop.

Ruth returned to the dwelling and prepared for bed in the usual sequence. Undressing, folding, the brief prayers that asked for guidance, strength, and faithfulness.

She climbed into bed and pulled the covers close.

The sheets were cool, then warm. Across the room, Abigail's breathing was already slow and even. The house was quiet, settling into the silence that came when the work was done and the day was finished.

Tomorrow, the bread would be made. Hannah's hands now, not Mercy's. The laundry would be done, Eunice testing the lye by touch. The fine mending would wait in its basket by the window. The chisels would be sharpened, James bracing his wrist against the wheel's housing, steadying by structure what muscle could no longer steady on its own.

Ruth closed her eyes.

The house slept around her. James's chisel, the one Samuel had made, waited on its peg.

Ruth slept.

CHAPTER ELEVEN

Silence

The Morning meeting was brief.

Elder Thomas read the passage for the day, a familiar one, about the virtues of labor and the sanctification of simple work, and the household listened in the usual postures of attention. The women on one side, the men on the other, the arrangement unchanged from how it had been for a hundred years. The light came through the eastern windows as it came each morning. No one disturbed the air.

When the reading ended, Elder Thomas closed the book. The sound was soft, familiar, the leather settling against itself. He looked out at the assembled household and nodded once.

"The day is before us," he said. "Let us be faithful to it."

The household rose. The meeting was complete.

Ruth noticed, as she had begun to notice over the past weeks, that no one spoke afterward. There had been a time, not so long ago, really, though it felt longer now, when the ending of the morning meeting had prompted small exchanges. A word about the reading. A question about the day's work. A comment, perhaps, on the weather or the progress of some seasonal task. These were not violations of order; they were the small breath of community, the evidence that people lived together and thought together and carried their thoughts into shared air.

Now the household dispersed in silence. Not the intentional silence of the meeting itself, the held quiet that was part of the practice, but a different kind. The silence of people who had nothing that needed to be said.

Ruth watched them go. Mercy to the kitchen. Hannah following. Abigail toward the dairy. Eunice to whatever work the day had assigned her. Brother Joseph to the woodshed. The others to their appointed places. Each body moving in its proper direction, each face composed, each mouth closed.

She did not follow them immediately. Instead, she remained in the meeting room after the others had left, standing alone in the space that had just held the household's morning gathering.

Eleven chairs. Eleven places arranged in the familiar pattern, the women's side and the men's side, the aisle between them, Elder Thomas's seat at the head. The arrangement was correct. The arrangement had always been correct.

But the room was wrong for eleven chairs.

Ruth looked up at the ceiling, at the height that made no sense for a room where people sat and listened to readings. The ceiling soared. The beams were thick, built to bear the weight that sitting bodies did not create. The walls rose and then angled inward, shaped in a way that would carry sound, that would gather voices and return them amplified to the ears of those who had made them.

The room had been built for forty. Ruth knew this. Everyone knew this in the way that everyone knew things that were never discussed. The community had once been larger. The room had been sized for that larger community. The explanation was simple, practical, requiring no further thought.

But standing alone in the empty space, Ruth felt something else. The room had not been built for forty people sitting. The room had been built for forty people moving. The ceiling was high enough for arms to raise, for bodies to reach upward without striking the beams. The floor beneath her feet was thick, solid, constructed to absorb the impact of stamping, of jumping, of the particular percussion that happened when many bodies moved in unison. The walls were angled to carry sound because the sound they were meant to carry was not the quiet voice of a single reader. The sound was singing. The sound was crying out. The sound was whatever noise emerged from throats when the spirit moved through them and demanded expression.

The room was a container. Ruth understood this now, standing in its emptiness. The room had been built to hold something that required holding. The proportions that seemed excessive for eleven people sitting still were exactly right for forty people in motion, forty bodies shaking and swaying and stamping and raising their arms toward a ceiling that had been placed precisely high enough to receive the gesture.

The room remembered what it had been built for. The room waited, patient and empty, for what would not come.

Ruth stood in the center of the floor, in the space between the women's chairs and the men's chairs, the space that was now simply an aisle for walking but had once been something else. She looked down at the worn wood beneath her feet. The wear patterns here were different from the wear patterns near the chairs. The wood was smoother, more evenly abraded, as if many feet had moved across it in many directions, not walking but doing something else, something that required the whole body and left its evidence in the grain.

She did not stay long. There was work to do. There was always work to do.

But as she left the meeting room, she carried with her the feeling of the space, the wrongness of the proportions, the architecture that made no sense unless you knew what had once happened within it. Eleven chairs in a room built for forty bodies in motion. The container remained. What it had contained was gone.

The kitchen was warm, the fire already built up, the morning's work underway. Ruth stood in the doorway and watched, as she had come to watch, noting the rhythm of the labor without interrupting it.

Hannah was at the stove, stirring the oats. Her hands moved with the certainty that weeks of primary responsibility had given her. Mercy sat at the work table, her attention focused on the dried beans she was sorting, her movements slow but precise. Neither of them spoke.

This too had changed. There had been a time when the kitchen held conversation. Not idle talk, not distraction from the work, but the ordinary exchange that happened when people labored in shared space. Observations about the food. Questions about quantities. Small negotiations about timing and sequence. The words had been functional, necessary, part of how the work organized itself.

Now the kitchen held only the sounds of the work itself. The scrape of the spoon against the pot. The soft click of beans sorted into bowls. The crackle of the fire. The sounds were sufficient. The sounds were all that was needed.

Ruth entered and began her morning inspection, moving through the stations as she moved each morning, checking what was present and what would need attention. The bread was rising. The preserves were stocked. The dried herbs hung in their proper bundles.

"The oats will be ready soon," Hannah said, the first words spoken since Ruth had arrived.

"Good," Ruth said.

The conversation ended. Hannah returned to her stirring. Ruth completed her inspection and left the kitchen, stepping into the hallway where the cold November air pressed against the windows.

She paused for a moment, standing in the quiet corridor, listening to the sounds of the household beginning its day. Footsteps on the floor above. The distant clatter of the laundry shed. The creak of a door opening and closing somewhere in the building.

The sounds were familiar. The sounds were right. But there was something underneath them, or rather, something missing from underneath them, that Ruth could not quite name. A texture that had been present and was no longer present. A density of small noises that had thinned without anyone deciding to thin it.

She continued her rounds.

At the dairy, Abigail was working alone.

The churning had begun, the paddle moving through the cream with the steady rhythm that the work required. Abigail's arms rose and fell, rose and fell, her body leaning into the motion with the practiced efficiency of long years. She did not look up when Ruth entered.

Ruth watched for a moment, noting the progress of the butter, the texture of the cream as it began to thicken. The work was proceeding. The work was always proceeding.

"Hannah will come to help with the lifting," Ruth said. "When the butter is ready to be gathered."

Abigail nodded without pausing in her churning. "I know. She told me yesterday."

The words were simple, adequate, and complete. Ruth waited for a moment, in case there was more. In case Abigail had something to add about the work, or the butter, or the way the morning was proceeding. There had been a time when Abigail would have offered observations. The cream is good this week, better than last. The cold helps the churning. It comes faster when the dairy is cold. Small comments that filled the space between tasks, that made the work feel shared even when it was done alone.

Abigail said nothing more. Her arms continued their rhythm. The cream thickened toward butter.

Ruth turned to leave, and as she did, she saw Abigail's mouth open slightly. The beginning of speech, the preparation for a word that was about to be formed. Ruth paused. Abigail's mouth closed again. Her arms continued their rhythm. The paddle rose and fell.

Whatever she had been about to say, she had decided not to say it.

Ruth left the dairy and continued her rounds. She did not ask what Abigail had almost spoken. The question would have required an answer, and the answer would have required explanation, and explanation would have required time and attention that could be given to the work instead.

The decision not to ask felt, in the moment, like kindness.

The confession hour came in the late morning, as it always came, the household gathering in the small room where such things were done. Elder Thomas sat at the head of the room, his posture patient and still, his face arranged in the expression of receptive attention that he had worn for these gatherings for thirty years.

The household sat in their usual places. Ruth was present, as she was always present, her role as witness and recorder requiring her attendance even though she rarely spoke during confession itself.

"We are gathered to unburden ourselves," Elder Thomas said. The words were formula, spoken at every confession, unchanged in living memory. "What is carried alone becomes heavy. What is shared becomes light. Let those who wish to speak come forward."

The silence held for a moment. The usual silence, the brief pause that allowed those with something to confess to gather their thoughts and their courage.

But Ruth noticed, as she sat in that silence, that it felt different from the silence she remembered. The silence of confession had always been full. Full of presence, full of waiting, full of attention to what might be spoken, what might be released, what might move through the room when the words finally came. The silence had been a container, like the meeting room itself, built to hold something that required holding.

Now the silence was simply empty. The shape was the same. The pause, the waiting, the gathered attention. But the content had drained away. The silence was not holding anything. The silence was simply the absence of speech.

Sister Eunice rose first.

She walked to the front of the room and stood before Elder Thomas, her hands folded, her head bowed slightly. The posture was correct. The posture had been correct for a hundred years.

"I confess impatience," Eunice said. Her voice was quiet, steady, giving nothing away. "I have felt impatience with the slowness of my own hands. I have wished for the work to be finished when the work was not yet finished. I ask forgiveness for this impatience, and I commit to accepting the pace that the work requires."

Elder Thomas nodded. "Your confession is heard. Your commitment is witnessed. Go in peace."

Eunice returned to her seat. The formula was complete. The exchange had taken less than a minute.

Ruth watched and felt something shift in her understanding. Not dramatically, not in any way that would have been visible to an outside observer, but perceptibly, the way a room shifts when a candle gutters slightly before steadying again.

The confession was correct. Every element was present. The naming of the fault, the acknowledgment of its weight, the request for forgiveness, the commitment to change. Eunice had spoken the words that confession required, and Elder Thomas had responded with the words that absolution required, and the transaction was complete.

But something was missing. Ruth could not have said what it was. Not precisely, not in words that would have satisfied a question. The confession had no story. It had no moment, no specific instance of impatience that Eunice was bringing into the light. It had only the word itself, impatience, offered like a token, accepted like a token, the exchange completed without anything having actually been exchanged.

Sister Abigail rose next.

"I confess distraction," she said when she reached the front of the room. "My mind has wandered from the work before me. I have thought of things that do not require thinking when there was work that required attention. I ask forgiveness for this distraction, and I commit to keeping my attention where my hands are."

Elder Thomas nodded. "Your confession is heard. Your commitment is witnessed. Go in peace."

Abigail returned to her seat.

Brother Joseph rose. "I confess weariness," he said. "I have felt the work as a burden when I should feel it as a gift. I ask forgiveness for this weariness, and I commit to receiving each task as an offering."

Elder Thomas nodded. "Your confession is heard. Your commitment is witnessed. Go in peace."

Sister Hannah rose next. She was younger than the others, thirty-five, the youngest in the household by nearly two decades, and there had been a time when her confessions carried a different quality. She had confessed specific moments of frustration, particular instances when her patience had failed, or her attention had wandered. She had told small stories of her failings, had located them in time and place, had made them real enough that the absolution meant something.

"I confess haste," Hannah said now, standing before Elder Thomas with her hands folded. "I have moved through the work without presence. I have completed tasks without offering them properly. I ask forgiveness for this haste, and I commit to bringing attention to each thing I do."

The words were correct. The posture was correct. The formula was complete.

Elder Thomas nodded. "Your confession is heard. Your commitment is witnessed. Go in peace."

Hannah returned to her seat.

The pattern continued. One by one, the remaining members of the household rose and spoke their confessions. Doubt, irritation, slowness, ingratitude. The words were different, but the shape was the same. A fault named. A formula spoken. A response given. A return to the seat.

No stories. No specifics. No disturbance.

Ruth watched and recorded, her pen moving across the ledger page where she kept track of who had spoken and what they had confessed. The categories were familiar. She had been recording them for years, had seen the same words appear again and again in different mouths. Impatience. Distraction. Weariness. The vocabulary of human failing, reduced to its simplest terms.

But something had changed. In previous years, in previous months, even, the confessions had carried weight. They had been stories, sometimes. I was impatient with Sister Abigail when she asked me to repeat myself. I was distracted during the morning reading because I was thinking about the work that waited. The confessions had been specific, located, particular. They had required attention to hear and attention to absolve.

Now they were tokens. The form was followed. The language was correct. But the content had been, not removed, exactly. Generalized. Smoothed. Made safe for speaking by being emptied of anything that might require actual examination.

Ruth recorded the confessions and said nothing. There was nothing to say. The confession hour had proceeded as it always proceeded. Everyone who wished to speak had spoken. The unburdening was complete.

Elder Thomas closed the gathering with the usual words, and the household dispersed to the work that waited.

The afternoon was quiet.

Ruth moved through the buildings, checking the progress of tasks, noting what had been completed and what remained. The laundry was drying on the lines. The dairy was clean, the butter wrapped and stored. The kitchen was preparing the evening meal. Everything was proceeding. Everything was in order.

She found herself noticing, as she moved from station to station, how little she was needed. There were no disputes to resolve. No questions to answer. No tensions to smooth. The work was distributed among the hands that remained, and the hands were doing what hands were supposed to do, and there was nothing that required her intervention or attention.

She turned from the kitchen doorway and walked to Catherine's room.

The room with the garden window was warm, the fire burning steadily, the light fading toward evening. Catherine was in her chair, as she was in her chair now, her hands occupied with the endless sorting of threads that had become her contribution.

"Good evening," Ruth said from the doorway.

Catherine looked up. Her face was calm, composed, the expression that had settled over her features since the move to this room. "Good evening. I have sorted another basket. The blue thread is set aside for the work shirts. The white thread, the fine weight, I have tested it, and some of it is still strong enough to use."

"Thank you," Ruth said. "The guidance is valuable."

She entered and sat in the chair across from Catherine, as she had sat many times before. The room was familiar now. The particular way the light fell, the arrangement of the furniture, the smell of the fire, and the dried herbs that Catherine kept on the windowsill. It was a comfortable room. It was a room where someone could spend their remaining time in peace.

"The house is quiet tonight," Catherine said. Her hands continued their work, moving through the threads with patient attention. "Quieter than it used to be."

"Yes," Ruth said.

"I remember when the evenings were fuller. More footsteps. More voices. The sound of people moving through the building, going about their business." Catherine's fingers found a tangle and began to work it loose. "Now I hear the building more than I hear the people. The settling of the beams. The creak of the floors. The sounds the house makes when it is holding its breath."

Ruth did not respond immediately. The observation was true. She had noticed it herself, the way the building's own sounds had become more prominent as the human sounds had thinned.

"The household is smaller," Ruth said finally. "Smaller households are quieter."

"Yes," Catherine said. "That is true." She set aside a length of thread that was too knotted to save. "I do not mind the quiet. I have never minded quiet. But I notice it. I notice when things change."

"What do you notice?"

Catherine was silent for a moment, her hands still moving, her attention divided between the threads and the question. "I notice that people come to see me and do not stay as long as they once did. Not because they are unkind. They are very kind; everyone is very kind. But because there is less to say. The conversations are shorter. The silences are longer. And when people leave, they leave more quietly than they used to leave."

Ruth heard the words and felt them settle into the space between them. Catherine was right. The visits were shorter. The conversations were briefer. Not because anyone intended them to be. But because there was less to fill them with.

"Is there anything you need?" Ruth asked. "Anything that would make the room more comfortable?"

"No," Catherine said. "Everything I need is here. The threads. The fire. The window." She looked up, her eyes meeting Ruth's. "And the visitors. Even when the visits are short. Even when there is little to say."

Ruth rose to leave. At the door, she paused and looked back. Catherine had returned to her sorting, her head bent over the work, her fingers patient and precise. The fire crackled softly. The room held its warmth against the November evening.

"I will check on you tomorrow," Ruth said.

"I know," Catherine said. "Someone always does."

The evening meal was quiet.

The household gathered around the long table, the food served in the usual order, the silence held except for the necessary words. Ruth ate and watched. The faces around the table were familiar. Mercy, Hannah, Abigail, Eunice, the brothers on their side, Elder Thomas at the head. Eleven people where there had once been forty.

No one spoke beyond what was required. Pass the bread. More water. Thank you. The words were functional, minimal, sufficient for the needs of the meal without being anything more than that.

Ruth helped clear the dishes, carrying them to the kitchen where Hannah was already heating water for the washing. They worked together in the quiet, Ruth drying what Hannah washed, the rhythm familiar, the movements automatic.

"The meal was good," Ruth said.

"Thank you," Hannah said.

The conversation ended. The dishes were finished. The kitchen was clean. The work was complete.

Ruth made her evening rounds.

The building was settling into stillness. She checked the doors, the windows, the fires. Everything was secure. Everything was in order.

She found herself walking back to the meeting room.

The room was dark now, the fire not lit, the windows admitting only the faint light of stars. Ruth stood in the doorway for a moment, then stepped inside.

The chairs were shadows. Eleven shapes arranged in the pattern that the morning had required, that tomorrow morning would require again. The space between them was darker still, the aisle that was simply an aisle now, the floor that remembered what feet had once done upon it.

Ruth walked to the center of the room and stood where she had stood that morning. She looked up at the ceiling, invisible now in the darkness but present, felt the height that made no sense for a room where people sat still.

The room was silent. The room had been silent for years, for decades, silent in the particular way that rooms became silent when what they were built for no longer happened within them.

And beneath the silence, or within it, or woven through it in a way that Ruth could not quite locate, she heard something else.

A hum.

Low. Barely perceptible. The kind of sound that might be blood in the ears, might be the body's own noise heard in the absence of other noise. But it did not feel like blood. It did not feel like the body. It felt like the building.

The hum was in the walls. In the beams. In the floor beneath her feet that had been built to absorb the impact of stamping and had absorbed it, had taken into itself the vibration of hundreds of bodies moving in unison over decades of worship, and had held that vibration the way wood holds what is done to it, the way grain remembers the forces that shaped it.

The building remembered. The building held, in its structure, in its material, some residue of what had once filled it. The hum was not sound exactly. It was memory. The memory of sound. The echo that remained when the sound itself had faded, held in the walls that had been built to hold it, released slowly, imperceptibly, into the silence that had replaced it.

Ruth stood in the dark room and listened to the hum that was not there.

She knew it was not there. She knew that buildings did not remember, that wood did not hold sound, that what she was hearing was her own body, her own blood, her own mind filling the silence with something because silence required filling. She knew this.

But she heard it anyway.

She left the meeting room and closed the door behind her. Her hand rested on the latch for a moment longer than necessary, holding the door shut, holding the hum inside, holding whatever was or was not there in the place where it belonged.

She did not tell anyone. There was nothing to tell.

Ruth walked to her room and prepared for bed in the usual sequence. Undressing, folding, the brief prayers that asked for guidance, strength, and faithfulness.

She climbed into bed and pulled the covers close.

The sheets were cool, then warm. Across the room, Abigail's breathing was already slow and even. The house settled around her. Wood creaking, fire ticking down, the wind worrying the glass.

Somewhere in the walls, in the beams, in the wood that had held so much and now held so little, the hum continued. Or did not continue. Or had never been there at all.

In the morning, no one would ask.

Ruth closed her eyes.

They slept.

CHAPTER TWELVE

Absence

The chair by the fire was empty.

Ruth noticed this as she entered the meeting room for the morning gathering, her eyes moving automatically to the places where people usually sat. Elder Thomas at the head, his posture already settled into the stillness of waiting. The brothers on their side, arranged in the order that decades of habit had established. The sisters on theirs.

But Sister Abigail's chair was empty.

Ruth paused in the doorway, counting the faces, confirming what her eyes had already told her. Nine people where there should have been eleven. The absence was small. One chair, one body, one space in the pattern. But it registered in the way that absences register when routine has been long established. Something was not where it should be.

She took her seat without comment. The meeting would begin when it began, and Abigail's absence would be explained or it would not, and either way the day would proceed.

Elder Thomas opened the book and began to read.

The passage was familiar. One of the testimonies about faithful labor, about hands that served without complaint, about the blessing of work offered in the proper spirit. Ruth listened with the part of her mind that always listened, the part that had been trained over forty-three years to receive doctrine without resistance, to let the words settle into the spaces where words were meant to settle.

The reading ended. The silence held. The household rose and dispersed.

Ruth looked again at Abigail's empty chair as she left the room. It remained empty, as empty things do.

She found Abigail in the hallway outside the sleeping rooms, moving slowly toward the stairs with one hand pressed against the wall for balance. Her face was pale, her movements careful, the posture of someone whose body had demanded attention that could not be refused.

"Sister Abigail," Ruth said.

Abigail looked up. Her mouth opened, then closed. She nodded once, an acknowledgment that contained an apology.

"Are you unwell?"

"The cold," Abigail said. Nothing more. Her hand remained on the wall, steadying her.

Ruth waited.

"I will be at the dairy shortly," Abigail said.

"Take your time," Ruth said. "The work will wait."

But even as she said it, Ruth knew the words were formula. The work would not wait. The work never waited. And Abigail's absence from the dairy would mean that someone else would absorb what she usually did, would add her tasks to their own, would cover the space she had left without remarking on the covering.

Abigail nodded and continued her slow progress toward the stairs. Ruth watched her go, noting the careful placement of each foot, the deliberate transfer of weight from step to step. The body was doing what bodies did. Declining, withdrawing, reducing its capacity for the demands that life required. This was not illness. This was age, and age was not something that could be treated or cured or adjusted away.

Ruth turned and continued her rounds.

The kitchen was functioning when she arrived, but functioning differently than it had functioned before.

Hannah was at the stove, her hands moving through the familiar work of preparing the morning meal. Mercy sat at the work table, sorting through the tasks that her hands could still manage. The fire burned. The kettle steamed. The morning proceeded.

But there was a gap in the rhythm, a space where motion should have been and was not. The bread that needed shaping was unshaped. The vegetables that needed preparing were unprepared.

"Sister Abigail is delayed," Ruth said from the doorway.

Hannah nodded without looking up. "She is at the dairy this morning?"

"When she is able."

"I will cover what needs covering here."

The conversation was brief, practical, complete. The absence had been noted, the adjustment had been made, and the work would continue. This was how the household functioned. By absorption, by redistribution, by the quiet covering of gaps that opened without warning.

She made her notes and moved on.

The morning passed in small adjustments.

Abigail arrived at the dairy an hour after the meal had been served, her body finally willing to do what her mind had demanded. Hannah came to help with the lifting, as she had said she would. The work was done. The work was always done.

But Ruth, moving through the buildings on her midday rounds, found herself noticing the gaps more clearly than she had noticed them before. The moments when someone should have been somewhere and was not. The tasks that should have been completed but were not yet complete. The small delays that accumulated throughout the morning like snow accumulating on a roof. Each flake insignificant, the total weight eventually substantial.

She did not think of this as a failure. She thought of it as timing, as the natural variation that occurred when bodies aged and capacities shifted.

She continued her rounds.

In the early afternoon, Ruth went to check on Catherine.

The room with the garden window was warm, the fire burning steadily against the November cold. Catherine was in her chair, her hands resting in her lap, her eyes fixed on the window where the winter garden lay dormant and gray.

She was not sorting threads.

This was the first thing Ruth noticed. The absence of motion, the stillness of hands that were usually occupied. The basket of threads sat beside Catherine's chair, within easy reach, but Catherine was not reaching for it. She was simply sitting, looking out at the garden, her face composed into an expression that Ruth could not read.

"Good afternoon," Ruth said from the doorway.

Catherine did not turn immediately. There was a pause, a beat of silence, before she looked away from the window.

"Good afternoon, Sister Ruth."

"How are you feeling?"

"The same." Catherine's voice was quiet, measured, the voice of someone speaking from a distance. "The cough is the same. The tiredness is the same. I am what I am."

Ruth entered and sat in the chair across from Catherine. "The threads. You are not sorting today."

"No." Catherine looked down at her hands. "I finished the last basket this morning. I sorted everything that could be sorted, tested everything that could be tested, and set aside everything that was still useful."

"There is more thread in the sewing room. I can have someone bring—"

"No." Catherine shook her head slightly. "The thread I sorted. It will not be used. I know this now. The fine work requires the fine thread, and the fine work cannot be done, and so the thread will sit in its organized baskets until someone decides it is no longer worth keeping."

Ruth did not respond immediately. The observation was true. She had known it herself.

"Your guidance has been valuable," Ruth said. "The household—"

"The household has been kind." Catherine's voice was gentle, without accusation. "Everyone has been very kind. You bring me thread to sort, and I sort it, and the sorting feels like purpose, and we do not speak about what the thread is for." She looked back toward the window. "I am not complaining. I understand. There is comfort in useful occupation, even when the usefulness is uncertain."

"Is there something else you would like to do?"

"No." Catherine turned back and looked at Ruth directly, her eyes clear and calm. "I would like to sit by the window and watch the garden. I would like to remember what it looked like when there were people to tend it. I would like to think about the years I spent in the sewing room, and the stitches I made, and the garments I mended that have long since worn away to nothing." She smiled slightly, a small movement that held no bitterness. "That is enough. That is what I have to do now."

Ruth nodded and rose to leave. At the door, she paused.

"I will check on you tomorrow," she said.

"Yes," Catherine said. "Someone always does."

But as Ruth stepped into the hallway and began to pull the door closed, she heard Catherine's voice continuing behind her, speaking to no one.

"I had thought someone would come to learn the stitches. I had thought there would be time."

No reply came.

Ruth closed the door and continued her rounds.

The evening meal was served in the usual silence.

Ruth ate and watched. The faces around the table were familiar. Mercy, Hannah, Abigail, Eunice, the brothers on their side, Elder Thomas at the head. Ten people at the table where there should have been eleven.

Catherine's chair was empty.

Looking at it now, Ruth realized she did not know when Catherine had last eaten with the household. She did not know if anyone had brought Catherine's meal this evening, or if the task had fallen through the gaps that the day's adjustments had created.

She finished her portion. She watched the others disperse.

It was only then, standing alone in the emptying hall, that the thought arrived. Catherine. The meal.

At Catherine's door, she knocked.

"Come," Catherine's voice said, and Ruth entered.

The room was warm, the fire still burning, but the tray that should have held Catherine's evening meal was not there. The small table beside Catherine's chair was empty.

"Your meal," Ruth said. "It has not been brought."

"No," Catherine said. She was still in her chair by the window, her eyes fixed on the darkening garden. "I noticed. I assumed there was a reason."

"There was no reason. It was forgotten."

The word hung in the air between them. Forgotten. Lost in the gaps between one task and another, between one person's responsibility and no one's responsibility.

"I will bring you something now," Ruth said.

"There is no need." Catherine's voice was calm, without accusation. "I am not hungry. I have not been hungry for some time. The body asks for less when there is less it needs to do."

"I will ensure it does not happen again," Ruth said.

"Yes," Catherine said. "I know you will."

But as Ruth turned to leave, she saw something that had not been visible before. The forgetting was not an error that could be corrected by attention. The forgetting was what happened when a system had been stretched until there was nothing left to stretch.

She prepared the tray herself. Simple fare, adequate for a woman who was not hungry.

Catherine accepted it with a nod, setting it on the small table without looking at its contents.

"Is there anything else you need?" Ruth asked.

"No," Catherine said. "Everything I need is here."

The words sounded different now. Emptier, or perhaps more honest. Everything Catherine needed was here: the fire, the window, the chair, the room. And the meal that had been forgotten, and the thread that would not be used, and the stitches that would never be taught.

Ruth left the room and closed the door behind her.

Catherine died four days later, in the room with the garden window.

Hannah found her in the morning, still in her chair, her hands folded in her lap, her eyes open and fixed on the dormant garden. The fire had burned down to embers. The room was cold. She had been gone for some hours.

There was no crisis. There was protocol.

The household gathered briefly while Catherine's body was prepared. Elder Thomas read the passage that was always read at such times. The words were familiar. The words were sufficient. The household dispersed to the work that waited, because work always waited, and grief was not an excuse for the bread to go unbaked or the fires to go untended.

The burial would be tomorrow. Today, there was the room.

Ruth stood in the doorway of the room with the garden window and looked at what Catherine had left behind.

The chair by the window. The small table beside it. The bed, neatly made. The fire, now cold.

The room was not large. It was sized for a single person, for a life that had contracted to fit within four walls and a window and a fire that needed tending. Catherine had lived in this room for three weeks, and before that she had lived in the room on the second floor for fifty-one years, and before that she had lived somewhere else entirely.

All of that was gone now. What remained was inventory.

Ruth entered the room and began the work of cataloging.

The protocol was clear. Personal effects were sorted into categories: items to be redistributed, items to be stored, items to be disposed of. Clothing went to the general supply. Practical objects were evaluated for condition. Papers were reviewed, relevant information recorded, and the physical objects themselves destroyed unless they held historical value.

Nothing was wasted. Nothing was hoarded. What one person no longer needed, another person would use.

Ruth moved through the room with the ledger in her hand, noting each item.

Clothing, winter: two dresses, worn but serviceable. One shawl, wool, mended at the shoulder.

Personal items: a hairbrush, bristles worn. A small mirror, glass clouded with age. A Bible, pages soft from use.

The list grew. The categories filled.

A room emptied correctly was more unsettling than a death.

Ruth did not know where the thought came from, but once it arrived, she could not dismiss it. The death had been

Catherine's alone, private, unwitnessed. But the emptying was procedural, performed according to rules written by people who were themselves long dead. The emptying made the death official in a way that the death itself had not.

By the window, she found the baskets.

Three of them, arranged neatly on the floor. The sorted thread that Catherine had worked on during her final weeks. Blues in one section, greens in another. Each color gradation noted and grouped. The work of someone who had spent sixty years understanding how colors related to one another.

Ruth knelt beside the baskets.

Thread, sorted, three baskets. To sewing room for storage and use.

But even as she wrote the words, she knew they were a kind of lie. The thread would not be used, because there was no one left who could do the work the thread was meant for.

As she lifted the first basket, something slipped from beneath it.

A piece of paper, folded once, the edges soft with age. It had been tucked under the basket, hidden, or simply stored.

Ruth set the basket down and picked up the paper.

The handwriting was Catherine's, but younger. The letters were firmer, the lines more certain, the script of someone whose hands had not yet begun to tremble. The paper itself was old, yellowed.

She unfolded it.

A list of colors. Just that. No explanation, no heading. Simply colors, written in a column down the page.

Madder red Walnut brown Indigo deep Goldenrod Sage Madder red again Weld yellow Indigo pale

The list continued, perhaps thirty colors in all, some repeating, some appearing only once.

The colors were not alphabetical. They were not arranged by frequency of use or by the materials that produced them. Ruth could find no organizing principle, no logic that would explain why madder red appeared twice, and goldenrod appeared only once.

The list was arranged by something else. A sequence that had meant something once. A pattern that Catherine had understood and that Ruth could not read.

Was it private? A personal code, a way of recording something that mattered only to Catherine?

Or was it something else?

Ruth thought of the old dyers who had approached their work as prayer. Each batch made with intention. Each hue carrying a meaning the dyer had placed into it through the quality of attention.

Was that what this was? A record of colors made with intention, arranged not by their physical properties but by their spiritual ones? A sequence that tracked not what the colors looked like but what they meant, what gifts they carried, what prayers had been folded into them?

Ruth would never know.

The knowledge that would have explained the list, that would have made the sequence legible, that knowledge had died with Catherine. The paper was a fragment, a remnant, a piece of a pattern broken beyond repair.

She looked at the paper for a long moment.

Then she folded it once, along the original crease, and placed it back in the basket, beneath the sorted threads where she had found it.

She picked up her ledger. Thread, sorted, three baskets. To sewing room for storage and use.

She did not add: Paper found beneath basket, list of colors, meaning unknown.

The paper would go with the thread. The thread would go to the sewing room. And someday, when someone else cleared the sewing room, they would find the baskets and the paper, and they would not know what it meant either, and they would dispose of it or keep it, and the sequence would remain unread.

Ruth completed her inventory.

The room did not take long to empty. Catherine had accumulated little during her eighty-two years. By the time Ruth finished, the room held only the furniture that belonged to it: the bed, the chair, the table, the window.

Someone would need this room eventually. Someone always did.

At the door, Ruth paused and looked back.

The room was empty now. The room held no trace of Catherine. That was the point. That was what the emptying was for.

A room emptied correctly was more unsettling than a death.

The death had been Catherine's: personal, private, the conclusion of a particular life lived in a particular way. But the emptying was the community's. The emptying said: this is how we absorb our losses. This is how we convert a person into an inventory, a life into a list.

The emptying was efficient. The emptying was correct. The emptying was unbearable.

Ruth did not bear it. She simply completed it, left the room, and closed the door behind her.

She walked back to the office, her ledger under her arm.

She thought about the paper she had not recorded. The list of colors that would sit unread in the sewing room until someone found it and wondered, and received no answer.

She had not recorded it because recording it would have made it real in a way she did not want it to be real. As long as the paper remained unnoted, it remained outside the system, outside the inventory. It remained private, a secret between Ruth and Catherine and whoever might someday find it.

It remained, in some small way, alive.

Ruth closed the ledger.

The thread had been sorted. The colors had been arranged. The meaning had been buried.

Nothing had been lost that could be named.

Everything that could not be lost had been lost.

Ruth walked through the darkening hallway toward the gathering household.

She did not tell anyone about the paper.

CHAPTER THIRTEEN

The Task

The sewing room was cold when Ruth arrived.

The fire had not been lit. Hannah was already there, seated in the chair by the window where the light fell strongest, her hands occupied with something from the basket that sat beside her. The basket that had been accumulating for months. The basket that held the work no one remaining could complete.

Ruth stood in the doorway and watched.

Hannah's fingers moved with care, guiding the needle through fabric that Ruth recognized as the lace collar that had belonged to Sister Agnes. The collar had been torn along one edge, a small damage that Catherine would have repaired in an hour, the stitches invisible, the lace restored to something better than mere functionality.

Hannah was trying.

Ruth could see the effort in the set of her shoulders, in the way she held the needle close to her eyes, in the small pauses between stitches where she consulted something in her memory. She was following instructions that Catherine had given her, descriptions of how the needle should move, where the thread should enter, and how tight the tension should be.

The stitches were visible.

Not dramatically so. Not in a way that would be immediately apparent to someone who did not know lace. But Ruth knew. Ruth could see, even from the doorway, that the thread pulled slightly where it should have lain flat, that the spacing was uneven where it should have been precise.

Hannah looked up. Her face showed the particular exhaustion of someone who had been concentrating on something difficult.

"I am trying," she said. "The collar. Sister Catherine described the stitch. I am trying to do what she described."

"I can see," Ruth said.

She entered the room and crossed to where Hannah sat. The basket was beside the chair, its contents visible: the lace collar, half-mended; the silk ribbon with frayed edges; the woolen shawl whose seam had begun to separate; other items, smaller, accumulated over months of waiting.

Ruth looked at Hannah's stitches. Up close, the inadequacy was clearer. The thread was the right color, the right weight. The needle was Catherine's own, the bone needle worn smooth by decades of use. But the trying was faithful. The result was not the same.

"The repair requires—"

She stopped.

"Continue as you can," Ruth said. "I will return later."

She left the sewing room and continued her morning rounds.

The kitchen was warm, the fire built up, the midday meal already in preparation. Mercy was at the work table, her hands sorting through the dried beans that would become soup, her movements slow but precise. She did not look up when Ruth entered.

"Hannah is in the sewing room," Ruth said. "She will be late to assist with the meal."

Mercy nodded. "I can manage."

Ruth completed her inspection of the kitchen and moved on. The dairy, where Martha was churning alone, her arms rising and falling in the steady rhythm the work required. The laundry shed, where Eunice was sorting linens. Each station was functioning. Each task was proceeding.

She returned to the main dwelling as the midday bell rang.

The household gathered for the meal. Ruth took her place and ate in the usual silence, watching the faces around the table. Eleven people. Eleven bodies performing their roles, consuming their portions, maintaining the patterns that the community required.

Hannah arrived late, sliding into her seat with a murmured apology that no one acknowledged. Her hands, Ruth noticed, showed small marks where the needle had pricked her fingers.

After the meal, Ruth helped clear the dishes. The work was routine, automatic. She dried what Hannah washed, the rhythm familiar, the silence comfortable.

"I cannot finish the collar today," Hannah said, her hands still moving through the soapy water. "The stitches are not right. I have tried three times, and each time I must remove what I have done and begin again."

Ruth continued drying. "The fine work is difficult."

"Sister Catherine made it look simple. Her hands moved, and the lace was whole again. I watched her do it many times. But watching is not the same as knowing."

"No," Ruth said. "It is not."

The dishes were finished. Hannah drained the water and wiped down the surfaces.

"I am needed in the dairy this afternoon," Hannah said. "Sister Martha's back is troubling her. She cannot manage the lifting alone."

"Go to the dairy," Ruth said. "The sewing can wait."

Hannah nodded and left the kitchen. Ruth stood for a moment in the empty room, listening to the fire settle, to the building creak in the cold.

The sewing could wait. The sewing had been waiting.

Ruth walked to the sewing room.

The room was empty now. The fire was still unlit, the air cold, the light from the south-facing windows thin and gray. The chair where Hannah had sat was pushed back slightly from its usual position. The bone needle rested on the small table, a length of thread still attached.

The basket sat where it had always sat, beside the window.

Ruth crossed to the basket and looked at what it held.

The lace collar lay on top, Hannah's attempted repair visible in the uneven stitches that crossed the torn edge. Beneath the collar, the silk ribbon. Frayed at both edges now, the damage spreading slowly. The ribbon had been used for decades in the celebration of particular holy days. It had been carried in processions, draped over the speaking stand, handled by dozens of hands over dozens of years.

Beneath the ribbon, the woolen shawl. The seam had separated further since Ruth had last looked. The original stitching was too fine to replicate.

Ruth lifted the basket.

It was heavier than she expected. The accumulated weight of months, of items added one by one, of work deferred and deferred again.

She carried the basket out of the sewing room.

The hallway was quiet. The afternoon work was proceeding in other parts of the building. No one was here to see her walking with the basket, to ask where she was taking it.

The storage room was at the end of the hall, past the empty dormitory. Ruth opened the door and stepped inside.

The room held what the community no longer used but had not discarded. Furniture that had been replaced. Tools that had been superseded. Fabric that had been set aside for projects that were never begun.

Ruth found a shelf at the back of the room, between a stack of unused hymnals and a crate of candle molds. The shelf was empty.

She placed the basket on the shelf.

The movement was administrative. She set the basket down, adjusted its position so it sat squarely on the wood, and stepped back.

The lace collar was still visible, Hannah's failed stitches crossing the torn edge. The silk ribbon lay beneath it, fraying. The shawl, the other items, all of it rested on the shelf, preserved but not completed.

Ruth left the storage room and closed the door behind her.

The hallway was still quiet. The afternoon light was beginning to fade. Ruth stood for a moment outside the closed door.

Then she walked back toward the sewing room.

The room was as she had left it. Empty. Cold. The chair by the window, the small table with Catherine's needle, the space where the basket had been. The space was visible now, a gap in the arrangement of the room.

Ruth did not adjust the furniture to fill the gap. She left the room as it was.

She continued her afternoon rounds.

The dairy was functioning. Hannah was there, helping Martha with the lifting, her hands occupied with work her hands could do. The laundry was proceeding. The kitchen was preparing the evening meal.

Each station was checked. Each task was noted.

The evening meal was quiet. The household gathered, the food was served, the silence held. Ruth ate and watched. The day was ending as days ended.

After the meal, Ruth made her evening rounds. The kitchen was clean, the fires banked, the doors secured.

She passed the storage room. The door was closed.

The sewing room was dark, the fire never lit. Tomorrow, Hannah would return to the kitchen, to the dairy, to the tasks that required her hands. The chair by the window would remain empty.

Ruth turned from the window at the end of the hall.

In the sewing room, the space where the basket had been held its shape in the dust.

CHAPTER FOURTEEN

The Record

The ledger lay open on the desk, the morning light falling across its pages.

Ruth had brought it from the small office to the meeting room, where the light was better, and the table was larger. The book was old, older than she was, its binding worn soft by decades of hands, its pages filled with the careful script of everyone who had held her position before her. The earliest entries were in a hand she did not recognize, the ink faded to brown, the language formal in ways that no longer matched how the community spoke. But the columns were the same. The categories were the same. Name. Role. Capacity. Status.

She turned to the current pages, where her own handwriting filled the lines.

The household inventory was due. Not required by anyone outside. There was no one outside who asked for such things anymore. But required by the practice itself, by the rhythm of documentation that had sustained the community since its founding. Every November, the record was updated. Every November, the state of the household was set down in ink, made permanent, made transferable to whoever might need to read it after.

Ruth uncapped the ink and took up her pen.

The first section was property.

She began with the land. The community held three hundred and forty acres, the same acreage it had held since 1842. The boundaries had not changed. What had changed was the use.

Cultivated land: 40 acres (reduced from 65) Fallow land: 85 acres Pasture: 30 acres Woodland: 185 acres (unchanged)

The north field had not been planted this year. She noted this: North field, fallow, insufficient labor. The notation was factual. She did not need to explain that the north field had once grown the best wheat in the county, that the loss of that field meant the loss of that knowledge as well as that labor.

The record required only the current state.

She moved to buildings. Main dwelling, meeting house, dairy, laundry shed: occupied, maintained. Sewing room: partially occupied. Carpentry shop: minimal use. The herb house, the seed house, the visitors' quarters: storage or disuse. She recorded each one with the same careful hand.

She moved to livestock and stores. Four cows, twelve chickens, no horses. Forty-two jars of preserved vegetables. Eighteen jars of fruit. Salt pork sufficient for four months.

Flour purchased, not milled. They no longer had the capacity to operate the mill.

The property section was complete. Ruth let the ink dry and turned the page.

The second section was membership.

This was where the record required care.

Ruth turned back several pages and looked at the membership entries from previous years. The list had been longer once. In 1860, the year she arrived, there had been forty-three names. In 1870, twenty-eight. In 1880, eighteen. Each year, the list had contracted. Not dramatically, not in ways that alarmed, but steadily, name by name, as the deaths accumulated and the arrivals did not.

She turned back to the current page and began with the living.

Eleven names now. Eleven, where last year there had been twelve.

Elder Thomas Whitfield, 75, 52 years, spiritual leadership, active

Thomas had arrived in 1845, a young man of twenty-three, drawn by the preaching of a traveling elder who had visited his village. He had given his life to this place. The entry did not record his sermons, his counsel, the way his voice could still fill the meeting room with conviction. The entry recorded only what could be measured.

Brother James Marsh, 67, 44 years, carpentry, maintenance, limited

James's hands shook now, a tremor that made fine work impossible. Limited. The word was accurate.

Brother Daniel Ward, 71, 48 years, general labor, limited

Daniel had not left the infirmary in weeks. His body was failing in the quiet, undramatic way that bodies failed here, not in crisis but in slow withdrawal. Limited. The word was generous.

Brother Joseph Ames, 63, 40 years, woodshed, mill, general labor, active

Joseph worked alone now, since Samuel's death. He stacked the wood and tended the mill and did the heavy lifting that the household still required. Active. The word was accurate, though Ruth could see the cost of it in the way he moved at the end of each day.

Brother William Hale, 47, 24 years, field labor, livestock, active

William was the youngest of the brothers. At forty-seven, he was learning tasks that had once been divided among five or six men. The entry did not record how quickly he was aging into work that was not meant for one pair of hands.

She worked through the brothers methodically, the pen moving in the familiar rhythm of transcription. Active. Limited. Reduced. The language was precise without being cruel. The language had been designed to describe exactly these situations. The gradual diminishment that age brought, the slow contraction of capacity that was neither failure nor fault.

She reached the sisters.

Sister Mercy Cole, 67, 41 years, kitchen oversight, reduced

Ruth paused at Mercy's entry. Reduced. The word was accurate. Mercy's hands could no longer hold a needle steady, could no longer knead bread in the cold mornings. But the word did not capture what Mercy still did: the sorting, the guidance, the small assistances. The word captured only what was lost.

Ruth wrote it anyway. The record required categories. A person was either active or limited or reduced or inactive. There was no column for "still trying." There was no notation for "doing what she can."

She continued.

Sister Abigail Warren, 46, 23 years, dairy, laundry, limited

Abigail had taken over the dairy work, had learned to feel the cream's readiness, to know by the sound of the churn when the butter was forming. The knowledge had passed to her through years of practice, through watching and doing and failing and learning. That knowledge was not in the record. That knowledge lived in Abigail's hands, in the practice itself.

But the mornings were harder now. The cold settled in her body and would not leave, and some days the walk to the dairy took longer than the work itself. Limited. The word was new to Abigail's entry. Last year it had read active. The change was small. The change was everything.

Sister Eunice Barlow, 38, 19 years, garden, laundry, domestic work, active

Eunice was still strong, still capable. Active. For how long? The record did not speculate.

Sister Hannah Reed, 35, 12 years, kitchen, general labor, active

Hannah was the youngest of them. Hannah would be the last. Ruth wrote her name and did not think about what that meant.

Sister Ruth Pelham, 62, 43 years, administration, coordination, active.

She wrote her own name with the same neutrality she had written the others. The words described what she did. They did not describe who she was, or what she remembered, or what she carried.

Ruth set down her pen.

The ink was drying on her own name. Sixty-two years old. Forty-three years of service. The numbers were correct. The numbers said nothing about what they contained.

She rose from the table and walked to the shelf where the older ledgers were kept. The volumes stood in sequence, each spine marked with a range of years, each binding worn to a different degree depending on how often it had been consulted. The earliest volumes were rarely touched now. The names they contained belonged to no one living. The entries documented a community that no longer existed except in the record itself.

Ruth pulled the volume marked 1858–1865 from the shelf.

The binding was stiffer than the current ledger, less handled, the leather still holding some of its original shape. She carried it back to the table and opened it to the section where new arrivals had been recorded.

The handwriting was Sister Eliza's. Neat, confident, the script of someone who believed the community would continue to receive new members, who kept careful record of each arrival because arrivals were expected, because the list would grow, because documentation was preparation for a future that would need to know who had come and when and why.

Ruth turned the pages until she found the year 1860.

November 1860. Three arrivals that month. The community had still been growing then, still drawing seekers from the world, still offering something that the world did not provide.

The third entry on the page was her own.

Sister Ruth Pelham, 21, arrived November 14, 1860, kitchen labor, active

Sister Eliza's hand had formed the letters. Sister Eliza, who had died in 1874, who had kept this record for thirty-one years, who had written Ruth's name without knowing that Ruth would one day sit where she had sat and hold the pen she had held and continue the work she had begun.

The entry was brief. Name. Age. Date. Assignment. Status. The categories captured what the categories were designed to capture. A young woman had arrived. She had been assigned to the kitchen. She was capable of work.

Ruth looked at the date. November 14, 1860. Thirty-seven years ago today.

She had not remembered, when she woke this morning, that this was the anniversary. The date had not appeared in her mind as she dressed, as she attended the morning meeting, as she carried the ledger to this room and began the annual inventory. The coincidence was not meaningful. It was simply arithmetic.

But she remembered the day itself.

November. Cold. The road from the town had been rutted and frozen, the wagon jolting over the hardened mud. She had arrived in the late morning, her single trunk beside her on the seat, her letter of introduction folded in her pocket. The letter had been written by a minister in her hometown who had known a family who had known someone who had visited the community years before. The chain of connection was thin. The decision to come had been her own.

She had been twenty-one. She had believed something.

Ruth could not now reconstruct exactly what she had believed. The belief had not been a proposition, not a statement that could be written in a ledger or copied into a doctrinal record. It had been more like a direction. A sense that life as she had known it was not sufficient, that there was another way to live, that somewhere people had discovered how to make labor into prayer and community into family and simplicity into grace.

She had read about the Shakers. She had read their publications, their testimonies, their accounts of the gifts that descended when the spirit moved. She had read about the dancing, the shaking, the voices that spoke through ordinary mouths when something larger than the ordinary moved through them. She had not known if she believed these accounts. She had known only that she wanted to see.

The wagon had stopped at the gate. A sister had come to meet her, had taken her trunk, and had led her up the path toward the main dwelling. Ruth remembered the path. She remembered the buildings rising around her, larger than she had expected, more numerous, the evidence of decades of labor made visible in wood and stone.

She remembered the meeting room.

The sister had led her past it, had not stopped, had continued toward the dwelling where Ruth would be housed and fed and introduced to the life she was entering. But Ruth had looked through the open door as they passed, and she had seen the room.

It had been full.

Not with furniture. Not with stored goods or unused equipment. Full of people. Forty, perhaps fifty, she could not count them, standing in rows, the women on one side, the men on the other, their bodies still but somehow expectant, their attention focused on something Ruth could not see.

She had stopped walking. The sister beside her had stopped too, had waited, had not spoken.

The room had been silent. The people had been silent. But the silence had not been empty. The silence had been full of something, charged with something, waiting for something. Ruth had stood in the doorway and felt the silence press against her like a hand.

Then someone had begun to sing.

A single voice, a woman's voice, rising from somewhere in the rows. The melody was simple, repetitive, a phrase that circled back on itself and began again. Other voices joined. The sound grew, not louder exactly, but denser, more layered, the voices weaving together into something that was not quite harmony and not quite unison but something else, something that Ruth had never heard before.

And then the bodies had begun to move.

Not dramatically. Not all at once. A slight swaying, a shifting of weight, a turning that began in one part of the room and spread like water finding its level. The movement was coordinated without being rehearsed. The bodies knew what to do. The bodies had done this before, many times, and the knowledge lived in them the way knowledge of walking lived in them, below thought, below intention.

Ruth had watched. She had not entered. She had not been invited to enter, not yet, not until she had been received and instructed and prepared. But she had watched, and she had understood that this was what she had come to find. Not the buildings, not the doctrines, not the separation of the sexes or the common ownership of property. This. The room full of bodies moving together. The silence that was not empty. The singing that was not performance. The labor of worship made visible in flesh.

She had believed, standing in that doorway, that she would learn to move as they moved. That the knowledge would pass into her body as it had passed into theirs. That she would become part of what she was witnessing, absorbed into the pattern, her individual motion joined to the larger motion until she could not tell where she ended, and the community began.

Ruth closed the old ledger.

The memory was complete. The memory was what it was. She did not know, now, whether what she had witnessed that first day had been the gift descending or simply the habit of bodies trained to move together. She did not know whether the silence had been full of presence or only full of expectation. She had been twenty-one. She had believed something. The belief had brought her here, had kept her here, had shaped forty-three years of labor and practice and documentation.

The entry in the ledger said none of this. The entry said: Sister Ruth Pelham, 21, arrived November 14, 1860, kitchen labor, active.

Ruth returned the old volume to its place on the shelf. The spine settled against the spines beside it, 1858–1865, between 1850–1857 and 1866–1873. The sequence was unbroken. The record was complete.

She sat down at the table and picked up her pen.

One entry remained to be completed.

Sister Catherine Shaw, 82, 56 years, needlework, deceased November 1897

Ruth's pen paused over the page.

Last year's entry had read: sewing instruction, fine needlework, limited. The notation had been accurate then. Catherine's eyes had been failing, her stamina declining, but she had still been teaching, still been contributing the knowledge that fifty years of practice had accumulated.

Now Ruth drew a thin line beneath Catherine's name and wrote the date. The protocol was clear. The deceased remained in the record for one year, their entry marked, their passing noted. Next year, Catherine's name would move to the separate section at the back of the ledger where all the dead were gathered, the list that grew longer each year while the list of the living grew shorter.

Ruth looked at the line she had drawn. Such a small mark. Such a complete erasure.

There was no place in the record for what Ruth remembered. The way Catherine's hands had moved through the fabric, finding the weakness in the weave by touch alone. The patterns she had invented. The paper with the list of colors that meant something once.

Ruth let the ink dry and moved to the next section.

The third section was projections.

Ruth turned back to the projections from 1860, the year she had arrived. The handwriting was Sister Eliza's, neat and confident:

- Projected membership increase: 5-8 new members anticipated

- Projected expansion: north dormitory renovation planned

- Projected labor capacity: strong, increasing

The confidence in those words was almost painful to read now. Sister Eliza had believed what she wrote. She had believed that the community would grow, that the future would be larger than the present.

Ruth turned back to the current page.

- Projected membership, next year: 9-11 (dependent on health)

The parenthetical was necessary. Of the eleven current members, two were in their seventies. Any winter could take them. The projection was not pessimistic. It was actuarial.

- Projected labor capacity: reduced (see individual assessments)
- Projected needs: external assistance for heavy labor, possible consolidation of living spaces
- No new admissions anticipated.

The words were simple. The words were true. No one had applied to join the community in eleven years. No one would apply. The age of gathering was over. What remained was the age of holding on.

Ruth let the ink dry.

The fourth section was doctrine.

This section had not changed in Ruth's lifetime. It was copied, year after year, from the entries that had come before. A statement of principles, a recitation of the community's founding commitments, a record of what the household believed and how that belief was practiced.

Ruth copied the familiar words:

We believe in the separation of the sexes as the foundation of purity. We believe in the common ownership of property. We believe in confession of sins and the pursuit of perfection. We believe in labor as worship and simplicity as grace.

The words came from Mother Ann's teachings, filtered through a hundred years of practice. They were the words that had drawn Ruth here at twenty-one, that had shaped her understanding of what a life could be.

After the principles came the citations:

Per the Millennial Laws, Section III: "All should labor with their hands..." Per Mother Ann's testimony: "Put your hands to work and your hearts to God..."

Ruth's pen paused.

She had copied this citation every year for twenty-three years. She had heard it spoken thousands of times. Put your hands to work and hearts to God. The words were as familiar as breathing.

But she heard them differently now.

The phrase had meant something once. The hands had not just worked. They had moved in ways that were given, not chosen. The work had come from the same place the dancing came from, the same place the gifts descended from when gifts still descended. The motion of the hands had been the prayer. The labor and the worship had been one.

Ruth looked at the words on the page. Put your hands to work. The instruction was clear. The instruction was what remained.

But hearts to God, what had that meant, when the bodies shook, and the voices cried out, and the gifts descended on those who were receptive?

The record preserved only the instruction, not the experience that had given rise to it.

Ruth completed the citation and moved on.

Per the Gospel Order: "Let all things be done decently and in order..."

The doctrine section was complete. The doctrine would outlast everyone who had lived it.

Ruth moved to the next section.

The fifth section was the summary.

She wrote:

North Family, November 1897

Membership: 11 (6 sisters, 5 brothers) Average age: 59 years Active members: 5 Limited/reduced capacity: 5 Inactive: 1

Deceased this year: 1 Property: maintained, some areas fallow Stores: adequate for winter Projections: gradual reduction in capacity; external assistance anticipated; no new admissions

The summary was accurate. Every word corresponded to a figure in the detailed sections.

Gradual reduction in capacity.

The phrase covered everything. It covered Abigail's mornings of pain, her slow walk to the dairy, Mercy's hands that could no longer hold the needle. It covered Catherine's death, the room that had been emptied, and the paper with the color sequence that Ruth had not recorded. It covered the fields that lay fallow and the buildings that stood empty and the skills that were being lost because there was no one left to receive them.

Ruth looked at the summary and felt something she had not expected to feel.

Relief.

The summary was complete. The record was complete. Everything that needed to be known was now written down, organized, and available.

It was easier, Ruth realized, once everything had a name.

Reduced. Limited. Inactive. Deceased. Fallow. The words were not kind, but they were clear. They did not require interpretation. They simply stated what was, in language that anyone could understand.

She let the ink dry on the summary page.

The morning had passed while she worked.

Ruth gathered her notes and returned them to the small office. The notes were no longer needed. The record had absorbed them, transformed them from observations into data, from memory into documentation.

She returned to the meeting room and looked at the ledger lying open on the table.

The book contained the history of the community. Not the full history, not the lived history, but the history that could be transmitted. The names, the dates, the figures. The slow contraction from a hundred members to fifty to twenty to eleven.

Ruth thought about Catherine. In the ledger, Catherine was a line of text: name, age, years, role, deceased. The line would remain. The line would be read by someone who had never known her, who would see the notation and understand that here was an old woman who had died.

They would not be wrong. The information would be correct.

But they would not know what the line did not say.

Ruth closed the ledger.

The binding was soft under her hands, the leather worn smooth by all the hands that had held it before. She pressed the covers together and listened to the soft sound of pages settling against each other.

The ink was dry. The entries were fixed. The record of the North Family for November 1897 was complete.

Ruth carried the ledger back to the small office and placed it on the shelf where it belonged, between the ledger from last year and the empty space where next year's continuation would eventually rest.

The spine faced outward, the date visible: 1897.

Ruth left the office and closed the door behind her.

The hallway was quiet. The morning work was proceeding in the kitchen, in the dairy, in the rooms where the household continued its patterns. The room with the garden window stood empty, its next occupant not yet determined. Catherine's baskets of sorted thread waited in the storage room, the paper with the color sequence tucked beneath them, unrecorded, holding a meaning that would never be recovered.

Ruth walked toward the kitchen to begin her afternoon rounds.

The ledger waited on its shelf, patient and complete, holding everything that could be held in language.

And releasing, into silence, everything that could not.

CHAPTER FIFTEEN

Joy

Elder Thomas sat alone in the meeting room.

The household had dispersed after the morning reading. The chairs stood empty on both sides. Five on the brothers' side, six on the sisters'. Eleven chairs where there had once been more than forty. The silence held the space the way silence always held it now, expanding to fill what voices no longer filled.

Thomas did not rise to begin his rounds.

He sat in his chair at the head of the room, his Bible closed on his lap, his hands resting on its leather cover. The light came through the tall windows and fell across the floor in rectangles that would move as the morning passed. He watched the light touch the worn places in the wood. The arcs and curves that made no sense for people sitting in chairs. That recorded something else. Something the floor remembered even if the people no longer did.

His eyes closed.

He had come to the village in 1846. Twenty-three years old. The world had offered him work and wages and the ordinary way of things, and he had refused it without knowing what he was refusing it for. Something in him had been waiting. Something had recognized this place before he understood what the place was.

The first morning, the bell had rung at five o'clock.

He had walked to the meeting room in a line of brothers, their footsteps falling into rhythm on the wooden floors, the sound of their walking filling the hallway with a pulse he could feel through his shoes. He had not known what waited in the room ahead. He had only known that the brothers around him walked as if they knew, as if their bodies had made this walk so many times that the walking had become part of them.

The room had been full.

Thomas had stopped in the doorway, his breath catching at what he saw. Forty-three people arranged on either side of the long space. Brothers to the left, sisters to the right. The distance between them was precise and unchanged, the bodies standing in rows that faced each other across the gap. No one spoke. No one moved. The silence was not empty. The silence was waiting.

He had taken his place among the brothers. An older man had shifted to make room for him, had touched his elbow briefly to guide him into position, had returned his attention to the front of the room where Elder Solomon stood with his hands folded.

The windows were tall. Thomas noticed this. The ceiling was higher than any ceiling he had seen in a building this size. Higher than it needed to be for people standing. Higher than it needed to be for any practical purpose. The walls were angled slightly inward as they rose, a geometry he could not explain, a shape that seemed to gather the space rather than simply enclose it.

Elder Solomon raised his hand.

The room began.

A single voice rose from the sisters' side.

The melody was simple. Four notes, then four more, a phrase that repeated and turned back on itself. Thomas did not know the song. He did not know any of their songs yet. He only heard the voice, clear and unadorned, filling the high space above them.

A second voice joined. Then a third. The sisters wove around each other, each voice finding a line that complemented without duplicating, each breath timed to enter where another voice paused. The sound thickened. The sound rose.

The brothers began.

Thomas felt it in his chest before he heard it. A low hum that built from the men around him, a foundation note that anchored what the sisters were building above. More voices joined, finding their places in the structure, adding lines that moved beneath the melody and beside it and through it. The sound was not unison. The sound was architecture.

Eight parts. Thomas would learn later that there were eight parts, that each voice knew its place in the structure, that the weaving had been practiced and refined until every singer could hold their line while hearing all the others. But that first morning he knew only that the sound was filling him, was filling the room, was filling the space between the floor and the high ceiling until the air itself seemed to vibrate with what they were making.

His mouth opened. A note came out. He did not choose the note. His body found it. Found a place in the structure where a voice was needed, found the pitch that fit between the voices beside him, found himself singing without knowing what he was singing or how he had learned to sing it.

The ceiling received the sound. The angled walls gathered it and returned it. The room had been built for this. The room was doing what it had been built to do.

The song continued. Thomas lost track of time. The verses moved through him, words about labor and faithfulness and the turning of the spirit, and his voice moved with them, held in place by the voices around him, part of something that required all of them and exceeded all of them.

When the song ended, the silence that followed was not empty. The silence was full of what had just passed through it. Thomas stood in his place among the brothers and breathed, and the breathing of forty-three people filled the room with a rhythm that was almost like music, that was the residue of music, that held the shape of what they had made together.

Elder Solomon's hand moved again.

A foot struck the floor.

Thomas felt it through the boards before he heard it. A single impact, sharp and definite, somewhere among the brothers to his left. Then another foot struck. Then another. The impacts came faster, finding each other, beginning to pulse.

The sisters responded. Their feet struck the floor on the off-beat, answering the brothers' rhythm, creating a pattern that wove between the two sides of the room. The sound was not music. The sound was percussion. The drum of bodies meeting wood, the floor becoming an instrument played by forty-three pairs of feet.

Thomas's foot moved.

He did not decide to move it. His foot struck the floor because the feet around him were striking, because the rhythm required another voice, because his body understood before his mind that this was not watching, this was participating, this was becoming part of what the room was making.

The striking organized itself. The scattered impacts became a pulse, then a measure, then a structure as precise as the singing had been. Each foot knew its moment. Each impact fell where the sequence required it to fall. Thomas's foot struck with the others, and the striking became a single sound, a single intention, forty-three bodies moving as one body.

The stepping began.

It started with the brothers. A shift of weight, a slide of one foot, a step that moved the line slightly to the left. The brother beside Thomas moved, and Thomas moved with him, and the brother beside that one moved too, and the line of men began to travel across the room in a pattern that was not walking, that was something more deliberate than walking, that had a shape Thomas could almost see.

The sisters moved in the opposite direction. Their line slid to the right as the brothers slid left, the two groups passing each other without meeting, the distance between them constant, the separation unchanged even as the bodies traveled through the space.

The figure turned. The brothers reversed, began moving right. The sisters reversed, began moving left. The lines passed again, closer now, the faces almost visible to each other, the breath of one side reaching the other, the heat of the movement beginning to build.

Thomas's body learned the figure as it performed it. His feet knew when to step. His weight knew when to shift. The movement was not complicated. Step, slide, turn, step again. But the precision required attention, required that his body listen to the bodies around him, required that he feel where the line was going and go with it.

He stopped thinking about the steps. The steps thought themselves. His body became part of the line, and the line moved as lines moved, and the turning continued.

The tempo increased.

Thomas did not notice at first. The steps came faster. The turns sharper. The foot-strikes harder against the floor. The sound grew. The floor absorbed the impacts and gave them back, a resonance building beneath their feet, a hum in the boards that Thomas felt in his knees, his hips, his chest.

The brothers' line began to curve.

The movement was still orderly. Still patterned, still precise. But the line was bending now, the ends sweeping around, the shape becoming a circle that turned in the center of the room. Thomas moved with it. His feet knew the curve. His body leaned into the turn, counterbalanced by the brother at his shoulder, held in place by the bodies on either side.

The sisters' line curved in the opposite direction. Two circles formed, turning against each other, the brothers moving sunward and the sisters moving against the sun, the space between them constant even as the shapes evolved. Thomas glimpsed faces across the gap. Eyes fixed forward. Mouths slightly open. Faces that were not smiling, faces that were intent, attentive, present to the work they were doing.

The circles turned faster. The foot-strikes came harder. The floor shook with the force of forty-three bodies moving in unison, the impacts building on each other, the rhythm becoming a pulse that Thomas felt in his blood. Dust rose from the boards. Fine particles catching the window light, hanging in the air like smoke, stirred by the stamping that would not stop.

He was sweating. The wool of his shirt clung to his back. The brother beside him was sweating too. Thomas could smell it, the sharp scent of exertion, the heat of bodies working in a closed space. The air was thickening. The air was growing close with breath and effort, and the warm animal fact of many people moving together.

His legs burned. Strike and lift. Strike and lift. The rhythm never paused. It offered no rest. It required the body to continue. Thomas felt the fatigue spreading upward. Thighs. Hips. The small muscles of the lower back.

He continued.

The brothers continued. The sisters continued. No one stopped. No one faltered. The circles turned, and the feet struck, and the rhythm pulsed through the floor, and the fatigue was not a signal to stop. The fatigue was part of it. The fatigue was the body being used. The body being asked for more than ordinary life required. The body giving what was asked.

The arms began.

Thomas felt it before he saw it. A lifting. A gesture that moved through the line of brothers like a wave. Arms rising in unison. Hands opening toward the ceiling that had been built to receive them.

His arms rose. The brother beside him, the brother beyond. All of them lifting together, the gesture spreading around the circle until every arm was raised, every hand was open, every body was reaching toward the high space above.

The arms fell. The arms rose again. The movement repeated. Rise, open, fall, rise. The feet continued striking. The circles continued turning. The rhythm continued to build. Thomas's shoulders burned with the reaching. The muscles across his back protested the repeated lifting. He lifted anyway. The pattern required the lifting. His body was not his own.

The sisters' arms moved in a different pattern. Sweeping gestures. Hands that traced shapes in the air, movements that mirrored and answered what the brothers were doing. The two circles turned against each other, arms rising and falling, feet striking, the room full of motion that was not chaos, motion that was order, motion that was order so complete that Thomas could feel himself disappearing into it.

This was the center of it.

He was not Thomas anymore. He was the turning circle and the striking feet and the rising arms. He was forty-three bodies moving as one body, breathing as one breath. The self that usually stood apart had no place here. The order was too complete to allow anything that was not itself.

His arms rose with the others. His feet struck with the others. His breath came in the rhythm the circle required.

Something shifted.

He was not performing the form. The form was moving through him.

And then it did.

A sister on the far side of the room cried out. Not words. A sound that rose from somewhere beneath language, that cut through the singing and the stamping and hung in the air like a struck bell. Her body began to shake. Not the orderly movement of the dance. Something else. Something that moved through her like wind through wheat.

The dancing did not stop. The circles kept turning. But Thomas saw others responding. A brother two places down began to tremble. His arms, still rising and falling with the pattern, shook with something beyond the pattern. His face was wet with tears he did not seem to notice.

The gift was descending.

Thomas had heard them speak of this. The elders, the older brothers, speaking in quiet voices about meetings where the spirit moved visibly, where bodies became vessels for something that entered and used them and passed on. He had thought they were speaking in metaphor. He had not understood they were speaking in fact.

The circle turned. His feet struck. His arms rose. And somewhere in the burning of his muscles and the dust-thick air and the pulse of the floor beneath him, he felt it reach him too.

Just a warmth that started in his chest and spread. A sense of being held by something larger than the room. A certainty that arrived without argument, without words, without anything he could have explained to anyone who was not in this room, in this circle, in this moment.

The tears came. He did not choose them. They ran down his face and into his collar, and he kept moving, kept striking, kept turning with the circle that held him, and the tears were not sorrow. The tears were overflow. The tears were what happened when something too large moved through a body too small to contain it.

The sound changed.

The foot-strikes softened. The turning slowed. The circles began to unwind, the curved lines straightening, the brothers and sisters returning to their rows on opposite sides of the room. The arms lowered. The movement stilled.

Thomas stood in his place. Chest heaving. Sweat running down his face. Legs trembling with the effort of what they had done. The brothers around him stood the same way. Breathing hard, faces flushed, bodies used in a way that ordinary labor never used them. Across the room, the sisters stood in their row, their caps dark with sweat, their breath visible in the suddenly cooler air.

No one spoke.

The silence gathered. Not the waiting silence of before. A different silence. A silence that was not empty but completed. The room held them in it. The high ceiling held the heat that rose from their bodies. The angled walls held the echo of what had passed.

The sister who had cried out stood quiet now. Her face was calm. Whatever had moved through her had moved on, leaving her standing in her place, breathing with the others, returned to herself but not unchanged.

Thomas felt it then. Not during the movement. During the movement, there had been no space to feel anything except the motion, the striking, the turning. But now, in the stillness that followed, something opened in his chest. A warmth that was not exertion. A fullness that was not breath. A presence that seemed to fill the room the way the sound had filled it, that seemed to hold all of them in a single attention, that made the silence not absence but arrival.

His eyes were wet. He did not remember beginning to weep. The brother beside him was weeping too. Tears running into his beard, his breath coming in small catches, his body still trembling but not from fatigue. Not anymore. Across the room, he could see sisters with their heads bowed, their shoulders shaking, their hands pressed to their faces.

Forty-three people standing in the aftermath of what they had done together.

Elder Solomon spoke. Thomas did not hear the words. The words did not matter. What mattered was standing in this room, in this body, in this silence that was not silence, feeling the thing that had descended when the turning stilled.

He understood now why the ceiling was so high. He understood why the walls were angled. He understood why the floor had been built thick enough to absorb the striking of so many feet. The room was a vessel. The room was designed to hold what they had made together, to contain the thing that required many bodies to summon, to give it a shape that would hold until the next gathering.

The meeting ended. Elder Solomon's hand fell. The rows dissolved into people. Individuals again. Separate selves returning to separate bodies, the form releasing them back into the ordinary morning.

Thomas walked out of the room with the brothers. His legs were unsteady. His shirt was soaked through. His arms hung heavy at his sides, the muscles still burning from the repeated lifting.

He did not speak. No one spoke. They walked down the hallway toward the work that waited, toward the labor that would fill the hours until the next meeting, toward the ordinary rhythm of days that would carry them from one gathering to the next.

But Thomas was not the same as he had been that morning. Something had broken open in him. Something had entered through the crack.

He did not have a word for it. The words he knew were too small. What he had felt in that silence after the movement stilled had passed through him like fire through dry wood. It had left him changed.

He walked to his assigned labor. He lifted, carried, and performed the tasks the day required. His body was tired. More tired than ordinary work made it. But the tiredness was not burden. The tiredness was evidence. And the work was easier afterward. Not because it was lighter, but because the body had been gathered back into itself.

Fifty-two years.

Thomas opened his eyes. The meeting room was cold. He could feel it now, the November air pressing against his face, his hands, the stillness in his legs where he had sat too long without moving. The contrast was sharp. A moment ago, he had been in a room thick with heat and breath and the smell of wool and exertion. Now he sat alone in a room that held nothing but silence and morning light.

His body remembered what his body no longer was.

He rose slowly. The movement was stiff, his joints protesting, his muscles cold. His body was seventy-five years old now. His body had performed that form thousands of times in the years after that first morning. Had learned every variation, every shape, every mode of the laboring dances. His feet had struck this floor until they knew its texture without looking. His arms had risen toward that ceiling until the rising was as natural as breath.

He walked to the center of the room.

The wear marks spread beneath his feet. Arcs and curves worn smooth by generations of turning, the wood polished by impact, the floor bearing the record of what had happened here. He could trace the grooves if he wanted. He could see where the circles had turned, where the lines had passed, where the most feet had struck in the most meetings over the most years.

The marks made no sense for eleven people. They were the memory of forty.

Thomas stood in the center of the worn place and looked up.

The ceiling waited. The ceiling had been waiting for years now. Waiting for the sound of forty voices singing in eight parts. Waiting for the heat of forty bodies moving in unison. Waiting for the thing that had descended when the movement was complete.

He could not give it what it waited for. Eleven bodies could not do what forty bodies had done. He had watched the meetings thin, the circles shrink, the movements simplify as the numbers fell below what the practice required. The same steps performed by fewer bodies. The same songs sung by fewer voices. The form remained. The fire did not descend.

There was a threshold. He had not understood this in the early years, when the community was full, and the fire came reliably. But he understood it now. Forty bodies could reach the threshold. Thirty could, sometimes. Twenty was difficult.

Eleven was not enough.

The forms continued. The household gathered every morning and performed what could be performed. They sang, though the singing was thin. They moved, though the movements were small. But the fire did not descend. The joy that had required many bodies to summon no longer had enough bodies to summon it.

He was the last one who remembered.

The brothers and sisters who gathered each morning had come after the fire had cooled. They had learned the forms without learning what the forms could summon. They were faithful. They maintained the movements with care. But they did not know. And Thomas could not give them what he knew. The fire could not be transmitted through language. It required bodies.

He had thought, sometimes, about telling them. He had not. What purpose would it serve? They could not reach the threshold. Knowing what lay beyond it would only make the not-reaching harder to bear.

Better to carry the memory alone.

Thomas walked back to his chair and collected his Bible.

The morning's work was waiting. Ruth would be making her rounds, her small book open, her notations tracking the labor that kept the household running. The brothers would be at their tasks. The sisters would be at theirs. The system would continue as systems continued, each person in their place, each task performed, each day carrying them toward the next.

He would say nothing of what he remembered. He would read the passages at tomorrow's meeting and sit in the silence and watch the household perform the forms they had inherited. He would maintain the order. He would embody the faithfulness that the community required.

And he would hold the memory.

The ceiling that had received the sound of forty voices. The floor that had absorbed the striking of forty pairs of feet. The silence afterward, when the movement stilled, and the gift descended, and the room held all of them in something that none of them had made alone.

It was gone now. It would not return. There were not enough bodies left to summon it, and there would be fewer bodies with each year that passed, and eventually there would be no bodies at all, and the room would hold only silence.

Thomas walked to the door.

He paused at the threshold and looked back. The light had moved again, falling now across the sisters' side, illuminating the chairs that waited in their rows. The room was patient. The room would wait for whatever came. Eleven people or forty. The diminished forms or the full ones. The order maintained or the order forgotten.

The room did not mourn. The room simply was.

Thomas stepped through the doorway.

Behind him, the light continued its slow movement across the floor. It touched the worn grooves where the circles had turned. It touched the arcs where the feet had struck. It touched the fine dust that still settled in the low places, the dust that rose now only when someone swept.

The dust was still. The grooves were dry. The light moved on.

CHAPTER SIXTEEN

Fidelity

The bell sounded at five o'clock, as it always sounded.

Ruth woke to the sound, her body responding before her mind fully surfaced. The room was dark, the November cold pressing against the windows, the fire reduced to embers that gave no warmth. The cold had a weight this morning. Not weather-cold but vacancy-cold, the temperature of rooms that held fewer bodies than they had been built to hold. Across the room, Abigail's breathing continued unchanged. The slow rhythm of someone who had not heard the bell, or who had heard it and chosen not to respond.

Ruth rose and dressed in the darkness. The motions were familiar: the layers of clothing, the pins and buttons, the cap that covered her hair. She had performed these motions every morning for forty-three years. Her hands knew them without instruction.

She walked to the meeting room.

The hallway was cold, the floorboards creaking beneath her feet. The building was quiet. The quiet of early morning, before the work began, before the household stirred into its daily patterns. Ruth walked through the quiet and did not think about what waited on the other side of it.

The meeting room was empty when she arrived. She was always the first, except for Elder Thomas, who was already seated in his chair at the head of the room, his Bible open on his lap, his eyes closed in prayer. She took her seat on the sisters' side and folded her hands.

The others arrived gradually. Hannah, then Mercy, then Eunice. The brothers on their side. James, William, Joseph. Abigail came last, moving slowly with her hand on the wall, her face pale from another difficult night, her body settling into its chair with visible relief.

Eleven people in a room built for forty.

The floor held wear patterns that made no sense for the way they gathered now. Arcs and curves worn into the wood by something other than walking, something other than sitting. Ruth did not follow the question of what had made them. She simply sat in her chair and waited for the reading to begin.

Elder Thomas opened his eyes and began the reading.

The passage was from the Gospel of Matthew. Ruth had heard it many times before. The words about faithful servants, about stewardship, about the master who returns to find his household in order. The words fell into the silence of the room and were received without comment.

"Well done, good and faithful servant," Thomas read. "You have been faithful over a little; I will set you over much."

Ruth listened to the words and understood them differently than she had understood them before.

Faithful over a little. The phrase had once meant: faithful in small tasks, faithful in daily work, faithful in the humble duties that made up a life of service. It had meant that no work was too small to matter, that every act of obedience was seen and valued.

Now the phrase meant something else as well. Faithful over a little. Over the little that remained. Over the eleven where there had been forty. Over the fallow fields and the empty buildings and the skills that would not be passed on. Faithful over a household that was contracting toward its end.

The meaning had not changed. Ruth's understanding of it had.

Thomas finished the reading and closed the book. No one disturbed the air. The household sat in the morning stillness, breathing together, present together, waiting for whatever the day would require.

Ruth did not pray for the silence to reveal something new. She did not ask for guidance or comfort or explanation. She simply sat in the silence and let it be what it was. The silence of a community that had gathered in this room for a hundred years, and would gather for however many years remained, and would eventually gather no more.

The meeting ended. The household dispersed to begin the day's work.

Ruth went to the kitchen to assign the morning tasks.

Hannah was already at the stove, the fire rebuilt, the water heating for the oats. Mercy sat at the work table, her hands resting on its surface, waiting for instruction.

"Sister Mercy," Ruth said. "The bread needs shaping. Can you manage it this morning?"

Mercy looked down at her hands. The hands that shook now, that could not hold a needle steady, that fumbled with tasks they had once performed without thought. "I will try," she said.

"If the shaping is difficult, Sister Hannah can finish. But begin with what you can do."

Mercy nodded and moved to the flour bin, her movements slow and careful. Ruth watched her go and did not offer assistance. The task had been assigned. Mercy would attempt it. If she failed, the failure would be absorbed by someone else. That was how the household functioned.

Ruth made her notation in the small book she carried. The book that tracked the daily assignments, the redistributions, the quiet accommodations that kept the household running. The notation was brief: Mercy, bread (limited). Abigail, dairy. Hannah, additional prep.

The words were the same words she had been writing for years. The system was the same system. What had changed was that Ruth now saw clearly what the words meant. Not just for today, but for all the days that would follow. Mercy's hands would not improve. Abigail's mornings would not become easier. Hannah would continue to absorb what others could not complete until Hannah herself could no longer complete it.

The trajectory was visible now. Ruth saw it, and she assigned the work anyway.

For a few minutes, the work settled.

Mercy's hands found a rhythm that held. Hannah's movements slowed, not from fatigue but from exactness. The room warmed as the fire took, the cold withdrawing without being noticed.

Ruth stood where she was and did not adjust anything. There was nothing to improve. The household was not full, but it was whole.

The moment held, then thinned back into the day.

She left the kitchen to continue her rounds.

At the dairy, Abigail was already at work.

She had arrived early, as she sometimes did now. Rising before the bell, beginning her tasks while the household still slept, completing what she could before her body demanded rest. The churning was half-finished, the cream already beginning to separate, the familiar sounds of the work filling the cold space.

"Good morning, Sister Abigail," Ruth said from the doorway.

Abigail looked up. She nodded once but did not speak. Her hands continued their motion on the churn, the rhythm steady despite the stiffness that Ruth could see in her fingers. The cold mornings were harder now. The body that had once moved without complaint required persuasion, negotiation, the slow gathering of will before it would do what was asked.

Ruth waited a moment, then asked, "The butter?"

"By midmorning," Abigail said. Nothing more. She would call for Hannah when it was time for the lifting.

Ruth nodded. "I'll let her know to expect it."

She stood in the doorway for a moment longer, watching Abigail work. The dairy had become Abigail's domain over the years. She knew its rhythms, its requirements, its small adjustments that made the difference between good butter and poor. That knowledge lived in her hands, in her timing, in the attention she gave to each stage of the process.

The knowledge would not survive her.

Ruth knew this. She had known it for some time, but she knew it differently now. Not as an abstract future loss, but as a present fact that required no resolution. Abigail would continue to make butter for as long as her body allowed. When her body no longer allowed, the butter would be made differently, or not at all. The transition would happen without ceremony, without acknowledgment, without anyone marking the moment when Abigail's way of working disappeared from the world.

Ruth did not say any of this. She did not offer comfort or recognition or the suggestion that Abigail's work had mattered.

"I'll check back before midday," she said.

She left the dairy and continued her rounds.

The sewing room was empty, as it had been for weeks now.

Ruth opened the door and looked inside without entering. The fire was unlit, the chairs arranged around the cold hearth, the baskets of sorted thread sitting where they had been placed after Catherine's final organizing. The room smelled of dust and disuse. The smell of a space that had been alive and was now waiting.

She did not light the fire. There was no one to use the room, no work that required its warmth, no purpose that justified the wood. The sewing room would remain cold until someone needed it, and no one needed it now.

Ruth closed the door.

She thought, briefly, of the years when the room had been full. Six or eight sisters working together, their needles moving through the fabric, their voices rising and falling in the quiet conversation that accompanied skilled work. She had been one of those sisters once, before her hands had been needed elsewhere, before the administration had claimed her attention. She remembered the satisfaction of a finished seam, the pleasure of work done well, the companionship of women who understood what they were making and why.

Those years were gone. The women who had filled the room were gone. Catherine was the last one who still held the knowledge, and Catherine sat alone in her room with the garden window, her hands empty, her teaching finished.

Ruth did not linger on the memory. The memory was not useful. What was useful was the present. The household as it existed now, the work that could still be done, the systems that still required maintenance.

She continued down the hallway toward Catherine's room.

Catherine was awake, sitting in her chair by the window.

The fire was burning. Someone had tended it, probably Hannah on her early rounds. The room was warm despite the November cold. Catherine's hands were folded in her lap, her eyes fixed on the garden where the last of the autumn light was beginning to strengthen.

"Good morning, Sister Catherine," Ruth said from the doorway.

Catherine turned her head slowly. "Good morning, Sister Ruth."

"Did you sleep well?"

"I slept." The answer was neither complaint nor reassurance. It was simply fact.

Ruth entered the room and sat in the chair across from Catherine, as she had sat many times before. The arrangement was familiar. The two chairs facing each other, the window to one side, the fire crackling softly in the grate. They had sat like this for years, discussing the household's needs, planning the work, sharing the observations that helped Ruth understand what was happening in the community.

Now there was less to discuss. The observations had been made. The understanding had been reached. What remained was presence. The simple fact of being in the room together, of occupying the same space, of continuing the practice of connection even when connection had narrowed to its simplest form.

"The household is well?" Catherine asked.

"The household is functioning. Sister Abigail is having another difficult morning. Sister Mercy is attempting the bread."

"Mercy's hands."

"Yes."

Catherine nodded slowly. She did not offer advice or concern. She simply received the information, as she had received information for fifty years, and let it settle into the understanding she had built over a lifetime of attention.

"The fire is good this morning," Catherine said. "Hannah tends it well."

"She does."

"She will be the one who carries things forward. When the carrying is needed."

Ruth did not respond. The observation was accurate. Hannah was the youngest, the strongest, the most capable of absorbing the work that others could no longer do. Hannah would be the last to need the carrying. Hannah would be the one who closed the final doors.

Catherine turned back to the window. "The garden is resting. It does that in November. Pulls everything inward, holds it close, waits for the spring that may or may not come." She paused. "I used to think the waiting was difficult. Now I understand it differently. The waiting is the garden's work. The garden is doing exactly what it should do."

Ruth sat with the words. She understood what Catherine was saying. Not about the garden, but about everything the garden stood for. The household was resting. The household was pulling inward. The household was waiting.

And the waiting was not failure. The waiting was what remained when fullness had passed.

"Is there anything you need?" Ruth asked.

"No," Catherine said. "Everything I need is here."

Ruth rose to leave. At the door, she paused.

"I will check on you this evening," she said.

"Yes," Catherine said. "You always do."

Ruth closed the door behind her and stood for a moment in the hallway. The conversation had been brief, unremarkable, the same conversation they had had many times before. Nothing had been resolved. Nothing had been repaired. Catherine remained in her room with her window and her fire and her memories, and Ruth returned to her rounds, and the distance between them was exactly what it had always been.

Presence without intervention. Faithfulness without rescue.

Ruth continued down the hallway.

At midday, Ruth sat in the small office and reviewed the week's records.

The ledger was open on the desk, the entries from the morning added to the running account of the household's activities. Bread shaped (Mercy, partial. Hannah completed). Butter churned (Abigail). Laundry begun (Eunice). The notations were brief, factual, the same notations she had been making for twenty-three years.

She turned to the membership page and looked at the names.

Eleven names. Eleven people. The same eleven who had been here yesterday, who would be here tomorrow, who would continue to be here until they were not. The names were familiar. She had written them hundreds of times, had tracked their capacities and contributions, had watched them move through the categories from active to limited to reduced.

She knew what each name meant now. Not just the role and status recorded in the columns, but the person behind the entry. The history, the knowledge, the particular way each one moved through the household's patterns. She knew that Abigail's mornings were harder in the cold. She knew that Mercy prayed longer in the mornings since her hands had failed. She knew that Abigail's silences were deepening, that Thomas's voice still filled the meeting room, but his steps were slower when no one was watching.

The record did not contain this knowledge. The record was not designed to contain it. But Ruth carried it anyway. Carried it alongside the official notations, carried it in the part of her mind that the ledger could not reach.

She had thought, once, that this knowledge set her apart. Now she understood differently. The knowledge was simply what remained when the record was complete. When Ruth died, the knowledge would die with her. That was not a tragedy. That was what it meant to be human in a system designed to outlast humans.

Ruth closed the ledger and sat for a moment in the quiet office.

The system would continue. The ledger would receive new entries. The categories would remain the same, and new names would move through them, and eventually all the names would be gone, and the ledger would sit on its shelf holding the record of people no one remembered.

She had understood it since completing the annual inventory, since writing the summary that explained enough, since closing the book and placing it on the shelf beside the years that had come before.

And she would continue anyway.

Not because she had no choice. She had a choice. She had always had a choice. She could have left at twenty-one, when she first arrived, and the life seemed strange and demanding. She could have left at thirty, when the community began to contract, and the future became uncertain. She could have left at any point in the forty-three years since, could have walked away from the bells and the schedules and the careful maintenance of a household that was slowly disappearing.

She had not left. She would not leave.

The choice was not made once and settled. The choice was made every morning when the bell rang, and she rose to answer it. The choice was made every time she assigned the work, every time she made her rounds, every time she sat with Catherine or checked on Abigail or recorded the day's activities in the ledger that would outlast them all.

Faithfulness was no longer automatic. It was chosen.

Ruth opened the ledger again and turned to the page for tomorrow's assignments. The work needed to be planned. The tasks needed to be distributed. The household needed to be maintained for another day.

She picked up her pen and began to write.

The afternoon passed in the usual rhythm.

Ruth completed her circuit. The kitchen, the dairy, the laundry shed, and the rooms where the household continued its work. She checked on Abigail, who was resting after the morning's churning. She spoke briefly with Eunice about the week's washing. She stopped at the carpentry shop, where Brother James was attempting a repair that his shaking hands could barely manage.

At each stop, she observed and noted and moved on. She did not intervene where intervention was not requested. She did not offer comfort where comfort would not help. She simply witnessed. The work being done, the work not being done, the quiet accommodations that kept the household functioning.

The afternoon light began to fade. The November sun set early, pulling the warmth from the air, drawing the household toward the evening routines that would carry them into the night.

Ruth returned to the small office to finalize the day's records.

The notations were complete. The assignments for tomorrow were planned. The ledger was current, accurate, and ready for whatever the next day would bring.

She closed the book and placed it in its drawer.

The office was quiet. The building was settling into the stillness that came with evening. The creak of beams, the whisper of wind against windows, the muffled sounds of people moving through their final tasks. Somewhere, Hannah was preparing the evening meal. Somewhere, Abigail was resting after her morning's work. Somewhere, Catherine was sitting by her window, watching the darkness gather over the garden.

All of it was continuing. All of it would continue tomorrow.

Ruth rose from the desk and walked to the door of the office. She paused with her hand on the frame, looking back at the room she had occupied for twenty-three years. The desk, the chair, the shelf where the ledgers waited in their ordered rows.

The room would outlast her. The desk would be used by someone else, or by no one. The ledgers would remain on their shelf, recording the history of a community that had gathered and worked and worshipped and slowly diminished into silence.

She had added her portion to that record. She would continue adding to it for as long as she was able. And when she was no longer able, the record would continue without her. Complete, self-sufficient, holding everything that could be held in language.

Ruth turned off the lamp and left the office.

The evening meal was quiet, as evening meals had become.

Eleven people at a table built for twenty. The food was simple. Soup, bread, preserved vegetables from the cellar stores. The silence held, broken only by the soft sounds of eating, the occasional request for bread or water, the scrape of spoons against bowls.

Ruth ate and watched the faces around the table. Each face was familiar, known, understood in ways that the record could not capture. She had shared meals with these people for decades. She had watched them age, had seen their capacities change, had recorded their transitions from one category to another. She knew them as the ledger knew them. Name, role, status. And she knew them as the ledger could not know them. As people who had chosen this life and continued to choose it, morning after morning, year after year.

The meal ended. The dishes were cleared. The household dispersed to the evening tasks. The banking of fires, the securing of doors, the small rituals of preparation that preceded sleep.

Ruth completed her final circuit.

She checked the kitchen, where Hannah was finishing the last of the washing. She checked the meeting room, where the chairs stood empty in the darkness. She checked the doors and windows, confirming that the building was secure against the November night.

At Catherine's door, she paused and knocked softly.

"Come," Catherine's voice said, and Ruth entered.

The room was warm, the fire still burning, the evening meal's tray sitting untouched on the small table. Catherine was in her chair, her eyes fixed on the window where the stars were beginning to appear above the frozen garden.

"You didn't eat," Ruth said.

"I wasn't hungry."

Ruth did not press. She did not remind Catherine of the importance of eating, did not offer to bring something different, and did not express concern about what the loss of appetite might mean. She simply noted the untouched tray and let the observation settle into the understanding she carried.

"Is there anything you need before I retire?"

"No." Catherine turned from the window and looked at Ruth directly. Her eyes were clear, calm, holding the same steady attention they had always held. "You've been faithful, Ruth. All these years. You've done what needed to be done."

Ruth did not know how to respond. The words were not a question, not a compliment, not a farewell. They were simply an observation. An acknowledgment of what Ruth had been and what she had done and what she would continue to do.

"I have tried," Ruth said.

"You have succeeded." Catherine turned back to the window. "That's rarer than you know."

Ruth stood in the doorway for a moment longer, watching Catherine's profile against the darkening glass. Then she stepped back and pulled the door closed.

The hallway was quiet. The building was settling into sleep.

Ruth returned to her room and prepared for bed.

The routine was familiar. Undressing, folding, the brief prayers that asked for guidance, strength, and faithfulness. The prayers were the same prayers she had said for forty-three years, the same words moving through her mind in the same order, requesting the same things.

But the prayers felt different now. Not empty. The words still meant what they had always meant. But conscious. Chosen. Each word spoken with the awareness that she could have chosen not to speak it, that the prayer was not automatic but deliberate, that her faithfulness was not a given but an act.

She finished the prayers and climbed into bed.

Across the room, Abigail's breathing was slow and even. The breath of someone who had withdrawn into whatever interior space she now occupied, who participated in the household's patterns only when participation required nothing of her. Ruth listened to the breathing and did not try to reach across the distance it represented.

The room was dark. The building was quiet. The household was at rest.

Tomorrow the bell would ring at five o'clock. Tomorrow Ruth would rise, dress, and walk to the meeting room. Tomorrow, she would assign the work, complete her circuit, and record the day's activities in the ledger that would outlast them all.

Tomorrow she would choose again.

Not because she had to. Because she believed.

The belief had not changed. The belief was the same belief that had drawn her here at twenty-one, that had sustained her through forty-three years of bells and schedules and quiet maintenance. She believed in the separation that preserved purity. She believed in the labor that constituted worship. She believed in the community that had gathered her in and given her a place and a purpose and a way to live.

The belief remained. What had changed was that she now held it with open eyes.

She saw the costs. She saw the erasures. She saw the system completing its work, reducing the complex to the categorical, preparing to continue without anyone who had lived inside it. She saw all of this, and she believed anyway.

That was what faithfulness meant when clarity arrived.

Ruth closed her eyes.

The house held its silence around her. The silence of a community at rest, the silence of people who would choose it again tomorrow.

She breathed.

She slept.

CHAPTER SEVENTEEN

The Sealing

The letter arrived on a Tuesday in March.

Ruth found it in the morning post, among the invoices for flour and the quarterly notice from the county assessor. The envelope was plain, the handwriting unfamiliar, the return address the Ministry at New Lebanon. She set it aside until after the morning meeting, until after the household had dispersed to their work, until the office was quiet and the light from the window fell evenly across the desk.

The letter was brief.

It acknowledged receipt of the North Family's annual report. It noted the membership figure: eleven. It noted the average age: fifty-nine years. It noted the projection: no new admissions anticipated.

It referenced Section 7 of the Covenant of 1830.

Ruth read the reference twice. Then she rose from the desk and crossed to the cabinet where the founding documents were kept.

The cabinet was oak, built in 1793, the wood dark with age and handling. The documents inside were arranged by category: property deeds, covenant agreements, governance protocols, and correspondence with the Ministry. Ruth had consulted these papers perhaps a dozen times in her forty-three years of service. The protocols were clear. The rules were known. There was rarely a need to return to the source.

She found the Covenant of 1830 in its proper place; the paper still sound despite its age, the ink faded but legible. She carried it to the desk and unfolded it beneath the window light.

The document was familiar. She had read it when she first assumed her position, had copied relevant sections into the administrative manual, and had understood its provisions as the framework within which the community operated. The Covenant established the terms of membership, the distribution of property, the procedures for governance, the relationship between the North Family and the Ministry at New Lebanon.

Section 7 addressed conditions of dissolution.

Ruth read the section slowly, her finger tracing the lines.

When the membership of any Family shall fall below the number necessary for the maintenance of Gospel Order, and when the average age of the remaining members shall exceed sixty-five years, and when no new admissions shall have occurred within a period of ten years, the Family shall be considered to have entered a state of honorable completion.

In such condition, the remaining members shall continue in their labors and their faith until such time as the Family can no longer sustain itself. The property and holdings of the Family shall then pass to the Ministry for disposition according to the principles of common ownership.

This provision is not a dissolution but a fulfillment. The Family that completes its work in good order has not failed but has finished.

Ruth read the section again.

The conditions were precise. Membership below the number necessary for Gospel Order. The Millennial Laws specified that number as twelve for the maintenance of full worship practice. The North Family had eleven.

Average age exceeding sixty-five years. The current average was fifty-nine.

Ruth paused. Fifty-nine was below the threshold of sixty-five. But the provision read "shall exceed," and the Ministry had referenced Section 7 regardless. She read the letter again. The Ministry had not cited the average age as the triggering condition. It had cited all three factors together, the membership and the absence of new admissions carrying the weight that the age alone did not. The Ministry's interpretation was clear: the totality of conditions indicated honorable completion, not any single measure.

No new admissions within ten years. The last admission had been Hannah Reed, twelve years ago.

All three conditions were met, or met sufficiently in the Ministry's judgment.

Ruth folded the Covenant and returned it to the cabinet. She sat at the desk for a moment, her hands resting on the surface where so many hands had rested before.

The letter from the Ministry had not instructed her to do anything. It had simply noted the conditions and referenced the relevant section. The Ministry was not closing the North Family. The Ministry was acknowledging that the North Family had entered a state that the founders had anticipated, had named, had provided for.

Honorable completion.

The phrase was not grief. The phrase was not failure. The phrase was category.

Ruth rose and walked to the meeting room where Elder Thomas was reviewing the week's assignments. He looked up when she entered, his expression patient, his attention available.

"A letter from the Ministry," Ruth said. She handed it to him.

Elder Thomas read it. His face showed nothing that would have been visible to someone who did not know him well. But Ruth knew him well. She saw the slight settling of his shoulders, the small adjustment in his breathing, the way his eyes moved back to the reference at the end.

"Section 7," he said.

"Yes."

"You have consulted the Covenant?"

"Yes. The conditions are met."

Elder Thomas nodded. He set the letter on the table between them. The paper lay flat, unremarkable, the words visible in the morning light.

"The founders provided for this," he said.

"They did."

"They did not consider it failure."

"No. They called it completion."

Elder Thomas was quiet for a moment. His hands rested on the table, the fingers still, the joints swollen with age. He had given fifty-two years to this place. He had preached and counseled and administered and believed. The letter on the table did not erase any of that. The letter simply named the present condition in the language the founders had established.

"What is required of us?" he asked.

Ruth had anticipated the question. She had read the protocols while Elder Thomas read the letter.

"A notation in the ledger," she said. "The date on which the conditions were recognized as met. The reference to Section 7. The signatures of the Elder and the administrative sister confirming the recognition."

"And then?"

"We continue. The provision does not require us to cease. It acknowledges that we have entered a new state. We continue until continuation is no longer possible. The property passes to the Ministry when that time comes."

Elder Thomas looked at the letter again. "The founders anticipated this."

"They anticipated everything," Ruth said. "They built a system that could end as well as begin."

"Yes," Elder Thomas said. "They did."

He rose from the table and walked to the window. The yard was visible below, the buildings arranged as they had been arranged for a hundred years, the paths worn by generations of feet. The dairy was operating. The kitchen was preparing the midday meal. The work was proceeding as it had always proceeded.

"We will make the notation today," Elder Thomas said. "Before the evening meeting."

"Yes," Ruth said.

She returned to the office and opened the ledger to the page reserved for significant administrative actions. The page was mostly empty. The last entry was from 1889, when the Ministry had consolidated the Eastern Families and transferred three members to the North Family. Before that, an entry from 1876, acknowledging the death of the last original member who had known Mother Ann personally.

Ruth ruled a line beneath the previous entry. She wrote the date: March 14, 1898.

She wrote: Conditions of Section 7, Covenant of 1830, recognized as met. Membership: 11. Average age: 59 years. No new admissions in 12 years. The North Family enters a state of honorable completion per the provision of the founders.

She left space for the signatures.

When Elder Thomas came to the office that afternoon, Ruth showed him the entry. He read it once, nodded, and signed his name beneath the text. His signature was steady, the letters formed with the same care he had always brought to official documents.

Ruth signed beneath his name.

The ink dried. The entry was complete.

Elder Thomas returned to his work. Ruth returned the ledger to its shelf. The afternoon continued. The evening meeting was held at the usual hour, the household gathering in the usual pattern, Elder Thomas reading from the usual texts. He did not mention the letter. He did not mention the notation.

There was nothing to mention. An administrative action had been completed. The community had been recognized as having entered a state that the founders had named and provided for.

The household dispersed to their evening tasks. Ruth made her rounds. The kitchen was clean. The fires were banked. The doors were secured.

She paused at the window in the hallway, looking out at the darkened yard. The buildings were shadows. The paths were invisible. The community was preparing for sleep, as it had prepared for sleep every night for a hundred years.

Nothing had changed. The work would continue tomorrow. The bells would ring. The tasks would be assigned. The members would rise and labor and pray and rest, as they had always done, as they would continue to do until they could no longer do it.

But something had shifted. Ruth felt it in the quality of the silence, in the weight of the air, in the way the building settled around her. The founders had built a system that could complete itself. The system was now completing itself. The notation in the ledger was not a decision but a recognition. The conditions had been met. The provision had been activated. Everything that followed would be execution, not discretion.

Ruth turned from the window.

The hallway was quiet. The doors were closed. The household slept or prepared to sleep, unaware that the ledger now contained a new entry, unaware that the words "honorable completion" had been written in the book that held their names.

They did not need to know. The knowledge changed nothing about tomorrow's work. The knowledge changed nothing about how the butter would be churned, or the bread would be baked, or the rooms would be cleaned. The system continued. The system would continue until it could not.

Ruth walked to her room and prepared for bed.

The sheets were cool, then warm. Across the room, Abigail's breathing was slow and even. The house was quiet, the silence no different from any other night's silence.

But the ledger on the shelf held a new weight now. The entry was fixed. The signatures were dry. The founders had provided for this, had anticipated this, had named it not failure but fulfillment.

The North Family had entered a state of honorable completion.

Ruth closed her eyes.

The house continued around her. The ledger held what the ledger held.

CHAPTER EIGHTEEN

What Remains

Ruth woke before the bell.

She woke as she sometimes did now, her body anticipating the sound before it came. The room was cold, the fire dead, the November air pressing against her skin as she pushed back the covers and rose to dress.

Across the room, Abigail did not stir.

Ruth dressed in the darkness, her hands moving through the familiar motions without thought. The layers, the pins, the cap. She had done this ten thousand times. She would do it again tomorrow.

The bell rang.

She walked to the meeting room. The hallway was cold, the floorboards familiar beneath her feet, the building holding its silence around her. She did not hurry. There was no need to hurry. The meeting would wait for her arrival, as it waited for everyone's arrival, as it had waited every morning for a hundred years.

The household gathered. Slowly, stiffly, the bodies finding their places in the arrangement that decades had established. Elder Thomas at the head, his Bible already open, his eyes already closed in the prayer that preceded the reading. The brothers, on their side, arranged in their accustomed order. The sisters on theirs.

Ten people in the room.

Ruth counted them as she took her seat. Elder Thomas, James, William, Joseph, Daniel. Mercy, Abigail, Hannah, Eunice, herself. Ten.

She did not count the empty chairs. The empty chairs were not part of the count. They stood where they had always stood, arranged along the walls, waiting for bodies that would not come. The chairs were part of the room. The chairs were not part of the household.

Thomas opened his eyes and began the reading. The words were familiar. Something about labor, something about faithfulness, something about the work of hands offered in the proper spirit. Ruth listened without following. The words did not require following. They required only presence, only the fact of sitting in the room while they were spoken, only the continuation of a practice that had been continued every morning since the community's founding.

The reading ended. The silence held.

Ruth sat in the silence and did not pray. She did not ask for guidance or strength or understanding. She did not petition for the household's welfare or the community's future or the souls of those who had gone before. She simply sat, breathing, present, occupying her place in the pattern that the morning required.

The silence ended. The household rose and dispersed to begin the day.

Ruth went to the kitchen.

Hannah was at the stove, the fire already burning, the water already heating. Mercy sat at the work table, her hands resting on its surface, waiting for instruction. The morning meal would be prepared. The morning meal was always prepared.

"The oats are nearly ready," Hannah said without looking up.

"Good."

Ruth moved through the kitchen, checking what needed to be checked. The flour bin was adequate. Enough for two weeks, perhaps three. The salt cellar was low but not empty. The preserves on their shelves stood in their ordered rows, the jars labeled in handwriting she recognized, the contents sufficient to carry the household through the winter.

She made her notation in the small book she carried: Stores checked. Adequate.

She did not write anything else. There was nothing else to write. The stores were adequate. Forty-two jars of preserved vegetables, the glass cool to the touch. The kitchen was functioning. The meal would be prepared, served, and eaten, and then another meal would be prepared, and the cycle would continue.

Ruth closed the book and moved on.

At the dairy, the door was open.

Abigail was inside, already working, her hands moving through the motions of the churning. The cream was separating, the familiar sound filling the cold space, the rhythm steady despite the stiffness in her fingers. The butter would be ready by midmorning.

Ruth stood in the doorway and watched.

Abigail's hands were slow but sure. The cold mornings made the work harder, made the body reluctant, but the hands still moved. The butter would be made. Tomorrow the hands would move again, or they would not, and the butter would be made, or it would not be made, and either way the household would continue.

"Do you need anything?" Ruth asked.

Abigail shook her head. Nothing more.

Ruth nodded and left.

She did not offer assistance. Assistance had not been requested. The work was being done, in the way it could be done, by the hands that could do it. That was sufficient. That had always been sufficient.

The sewing room door was closed.

Ruth passed it without stopping. She did not open it to check the baskets, did not look inside to see the chairs arranged around the cold hearth, did not note the dust that was beginning to gather on the surfaces no one touched.

The room had been closed for weeks now. No one had opened it. No one had suggested opening it. The work that had been done there was no longer being done, and the room that had housed the work was no longer needed, and the door remained closed because closed doors did not require attention.

Ruth continued down the hallway.

She passed the storage rooms where the extra linens were kept. Linens that had been made for a household of forty, linens that would never be used, linens that sat in their folded stacks waiting for bodies that would not arrive. She passed the empty sleeping rooms on the upper floor. Rooms that had been closed one by one as their occupants died, rooms that held only furniture now, beds made for no one, chairs facing windows that no one looked through.

The building was larger than the household that lived in it. The building would remain larger.

The midday meal was prepared and served.

Ten people at the table. The food was simple. Soup, bread, the last of the autumn vegetables from the cellar. The silence held. The meal ended.

Ruth cleared the dishes with Hannah. They worked without speaking, the rhythm of the task familiar, the silence comfortable. There was nothing to say. The work spoke for itself.

When the kitchen was clean, Ruth returned to the small office.

The ledger was where she had left it.

She opened it and turned to the current page. The entries from the morning were already recorded. The work assigned, the tasks completed, the small adjustments that kept the household functioning. She added the midday notations: Meal served. Kitchen cleaned. Stores remain adequate.

The words were the same words she had written yesterday, the same words she would write tomorrow. The system required the words. The words sustained the system.

She closed the ledger and placed it in its drawer.

The afternoon passed.

Ruth made her rounds. The kitchen, the dairy, the laundry shed, and the rooms where the household continued its work. She checked and noted and moved on. The work was being done. The work was always being done, in whatever form the day allowed, by whatever hands remained to do it.

At the carpentry shop, the door was closed.

Brother James had not come today. His hands had been too unsteady this morning, his body unwilling to make the walk from the dwelling to the shop. The tools sat where he had left them yesterday, arranged in their places, waiting for hands that might or might not return tomorrow.

Ruth noted the closed door and did not open it.

The absence had been absorbed. It was no longer an absence. It was simply the state of things.

At the laundry shed, Eunice was finishing the week's washing. The water steamed in the cold air. The linens hung on the lines, stiffening in the November wind, the white fabric turning gray in the fading light. Eunice worked without speaking, her hands red from the hot water, her face set in the concentration of familiar labor.

Ruth watched for a moment, then moved on.

The afternoon light began to fade. The November sun dropped toward the horizon, pulling the warmth from the air, drawing shadows across the frozen ground.

The evening meal was prepared and served.

Ten people at the table. The food was simple. The silence held.

Ruth ate and did not watch the faces around her. She had watched them for years. Had tracked their changes, had noted their declines, had recorded their transitions in the ledger that sat in the office drawer. She knew what she would see if she looked. She did not need to look.

The meal ended. The dishes were cleared. The household dispersed.

Ruth made her final rounds.

She checked the doors and windows. The kitchen still smelled of bread. The smell would be gone by morning. She checked the fires, banked for the night, holding their heat against the November cold. She checked the kitchen, where Hannah was finishing the last of the cleaning. She checked the meeting room, where the chairs stood empty in the darkness.

Everything was in order. Everything was always in order.

She returned to her room.

The room was dark when she entered.

Abigail was already in bed, her breathing slow and even, her presence occupying its corner of the space without requiring acknowledgment. Ruth undressed and folded her clothes in the darkness. She said the prayers. The same prayers, the same words, the same requests that she had made every night for forty-three years.

The prayers did not comfort. They simply were. Words spoken into the darkness, offered to whatever received them, completing a practice that had been completed ten thousand times before.

She climbed into bed and pulled the covers close.

The room was cold. The building was quiet. The household was at rest.

Tomorrow the bell would ring. Tomorrow the work would continue. Tomorrow she would rise and dress and walk to the meeting room and sit in the silence and receive whatever the day required.

She did not think about what tomorrow would bring. Tomorrow did not require thinking. Tomorrow required only arrival.

Ruth lay in the darkness and breathed.

The house held its silence around her. The building creaked and settled. The wind moved against the windows. The fires burned low in their grates, holding their heat through the long night.

Ten people slept in the rooms along the hallway. They would wake when the bell rang. They would gather and work and eat and rest and gather again, as they had gathered for a hundred years, as they would gather for however many years remained.

The system continued.

Ruth closed her eyes.

The darkness held.

Tomorrow the bell would ring.

CHAPTER NINETEEN

Return

The road was the same.

Margaret noticed this as the car climbed the hill toward the village. The last time they had come this way, they had been on bikes, the asphalt warm beneath their tires, the late summer air smelling of cut hay and apples. That had been. She counted back. Forty-three years ago. Riding north for no reason except that the weather was fine and they had nowhere particular to be.

"This is it," Edward said, slowing the car. "I think."

The buildings stood white against the November sky. The same buildings, surely. The same arrangement on the hillside, the same clean lines, the same sense of order that had struck her all those years ago. But different now. A sign at the entrance: Shaker Heritage Site. A small building that had not been there before, with a placard announcing hours of operation and admission fees.

"They've made it a museum," Margaret said.

"Apparently."

Edward parked the car in the gravel lot. There were two other vehicles. A Tuesday in November. Not many visitors.

They got out and stood for a moment, looking up at the buildings. The dwelling house rose four stories, its windows reflecting the pale sky. The meeting house sat beside it, smaller, simpler, its door closed against the cold. Beyond them, other structures. Barns, workshops, smaller dwellings. All white. All silent. All preserved.

"Do you want to go in?" Edward asked.

Margaret did not know if she wanted to go in. She did not know why they had come. They had been driving through New Hampshire, visiting their daughter in Concord, and Edward had suggested the detour without explanation. She had agreed without asking for one.

"Yes," she said. "We've come this far."

They paid the small admission fee to a woman in the visitor center. The woman gave them a pamphlet and a map and explained that most buildings were open for self-guided tours. The dwelling house. The meeting house. The sisters' workshop. The barn.

"Take your time," the woman said. "There's no rush."

They walked up the path toward the dwelling house.

The door was heavy, the hinges silent. Inside, the air was cold and still. The hallway stretched ahead of them, the floorboards worn smooth, the walls painted the same pale blue Margaret remembered from decades ago. Or perhaps she did not remember. Perhaps she was inventing the memory now, filling in details that had never registered.

Informational plaques lined the walls. The Shakers arrived in this region in 1792. At its height, the community numbered over three hundred members. The last resident died in 1923.

Margaret read the words without absorbing them. The numbers meant nothing to her. Three hundred people, then none. A span of years, then silence. The plaques explained and explained, and the explanations settled into nothing.

They walked through the rooms.

The kitchen, with its large hearth and iron pots arranged for display. The dining hall, with a long table set as if for a meal that would never be served. The small office, where a desk held a ledger open to a page of careful handwriting. Margaret paused at the ledger. The entries were neat, precise. Names and tasks and small notations she could not decipher. The ink had faded, but the words remained.

"Look at this," she said.

Edward glanced at the ledger and nodded. "Meticulous," he said, and moved on.

Margaret lingered a moment longer. The handwriting was small and even. The same hand, page after page. Someone had sat at this desk and written these words, day after day, year after year. Someone had believed the writing mattered.

She turned away and followed Edward up the stairs.

The sleeping rooms were small and spare. Single beds, narrow and hard. A chair. A small table. A window that looked out over the frozen fields. Each room was the same. Each room held nothing but the furniture and the silence and the faint smell of dust and old wood.

"Austere," Edward said.

"Yes."

They did not stay long in the sleeping rooms. There was nothing to see. The rooms had been emptied of everything except the furniture, and the furniture said nothing about the people who had used it.

They descended the stairs and left the dwelling house.

The meeting house was next.

Margaret pushed open the door and stepped inside. The room was large, larger than she had expected. The ceiling rose high above them, higher than seemed necessary for a room this size. The walls were angled slightly inward as they rose, a detail she noticed without understanding. Benches lined the walls, simple and backless, arranged in rows on either side of the open floor.

The floor.

Margaret stopped and looked down.

The floorboards were worn in patterns. Arcs and curves, rubbed smooth by something other than walking. The wear was heaviest in the center of the room, spreading outward in shapes that suggested movement, repeated movement, movement that had happened so many times the wood itself had recorded it.

"Huh," she said.

Edward looked where she was looking. "What?"

"The floor. The patterns."

He studied the worn places for a moment. "Dancing, maybe. I read somewhere that they danced."

"Maybe."

Margaret stood in the center of the room, in the place where the wear was deepest. She looked up at the high ceiling, at the angled walls, at the windows that let in the November light. The room was empty. The room was silent. The room held nothing but the cold air and the dust motes drifting in the pale sun.

She waited for something. She did not know what. Some sense of what had happened here, some residue of the lives that had filled this space. She felt the floor beneath her feet, solid and worn, and she looked at the ceiling that rose above her, and she waited.

Nothing came.

The room was just a room. The floor was just a floor. Whatever had happened here had happened and ended and left no trace except the wear patterns that could have meant anything or nothing.

"Ready?" Edward asked from the doorway.

"Yes."

They walked through the other buildings quickly. The sisters' workshop, with its looms and spinning wheels. The barn, with its ingenious arrangement of stalls and storage. The herb garden, dormant now, the plants cut back for winter, the beds marked with small signs identifying what had grown there.

At each stop, Margaret read the plaques and looked at the displays and felt nothing except the cold and a vague tiredness that might have been the drive or might have been something else.

They returned to the visitor center.

"Did you enjoy your visit?" the woman asked.

"Very interesting," Edward said. "Thank you."

They walked back to the car. The afternoon light was beginning to fade, the November sun dropping toward the hills, the shadows lengthening across the frozen ground.

Margaret paused at the car door and looked back.

The buildings stood white against the darkening sky. The dwelling house, the meeting house, the workshops, and the barns. All silent. All empty. All preserved exactly as they had been, or exactly as someone imagined they had been, or exactly as they needed to be for visitors who came and paid their fee and walked through and left.

She looked at the meeting house. The windows caught the last of the afternoon light. For a moment, the glass seemed to glow, seemed to hold something, seemed to offer something she could almost see.

Then the light shifted, and the windows were just windows, and the building was just a building, and there was nothing there.

"Coming?" Edward asked.

"Yes."

She got into the car. Edward started the engine. They pulled out of the gravel lot and turned onto the paved road that led back down the hill.

Margaret did not look back again.

The buildings grew smaller in the distance, white against the Belknap hills, holding their silence, holding their secrets, holding whatever they held. The road curved, and the buildings disappeared behind the trees.

Edward turned on the radio. A voice spoke about weather, about traffic, about the ordinary concerns of an ordinary afternoon.

They drove on.

A Note on the Shakers

The United Society of Believers in Christ's Second Appearing, known as the Shakers for their ecstatic worship, was founded in England in 1747 and brought to America by Ann Lee in 1774. At their peak in the mid-nineteenth century, between 4,000 and 6,000 members lived in eighteen communities from Maine to Indiana. They were sustained by celibacy, communal labor, equality of the sexes, and the belief that heaven could be built on earth through perfect order.

Canterbury Shaker Village in New Hampshire was established in 1792. By the 1850s, it held nearly 300 residents on 3,000 acres. A century later, fewer than a dozen remained.

The last Canterbury Shaker, Ethel Hudson, died in 1992. The village is now a museum.

One active Shaker community continues at Sabbathday Lake, Maine.

Further Reading

Stephen J. Stein's *The Shaker Experience in America* (Yale, 1992) remains the definitive history. Ken Burns's 1984 documentary *The Shakers: Hands to Work, Hearts to God* offers a moving visual record. Canterbury Shaker Village maintains an archive at shakers.org.

Author's Note

This novel is a work of fiction. Canterbury Shaker Village is a real place. The characters and events are imagined, but the questions they carry are not.

www.ingramcontent.com/pod-product-compliance
Lightning Source LLC
LaVergne TN
LVHW091713070526
838199LV00050B/2376